IMPOSSIBLE LOVE

When Maria goes to live with her half-brother on the Isle of Man, she finds employment as a lady's maid to the autocratic Mrs. Pennington. Maria finds herself becoming very attracted to the Penningtons' only son, Daniel, but fights against it as he is from a different class. She becomes engaged to Rob Cregeen, who takes a job in the Penningtons' mines. But when Rob is killed in a mining disaster, Maria blames the Penningtons . . .

CAROLINE JOYCE

IMPOSSIBLE LOVE

Complete and Unabridged

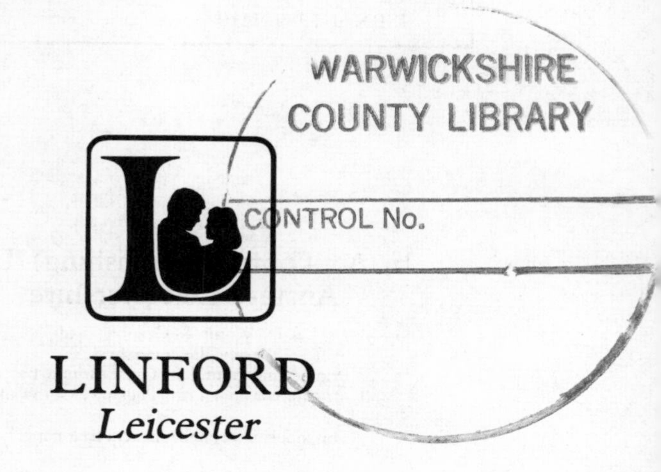

LINFORD
Leicester

First published in Great Britain in 1997
under the name of Shirley Allen

First Linford Edition
published 1999

British Library CIP Data

Joyce, Caroline
Impossible love.—Large print ed.—
Linford romance library
1. Love stories
2. Large type books
I. Title
823.9′14 [F]

ISBN 0–7089–5410–3

Published by
F. A. Thorpe (Publishing) Ltd.
Anstey, Leicestershire

Set by Words & Graphics Ltd.
Anstey, Leicestershire
Printed and bound in Great Britain by
T. J. International Ltd., Padstow, Cornwall

This book is printed on acid-free paper

SPECIAL MESSAGE TO READERS

This book is published under the auspices of

THE ULVERSCROFT FOUNDATION

(registered charity No. 264873 UK)

Established in 1972 to provide funds for research, diagnosis and treatment of eye diseases.

Examples of contributions made are: —

A Children's Assessment Unit at Moorfield's Hospital, London.

•

Twin operating theatres at the Western Ophthalmic Hospital, London.

•

A Chair of Ophthalmology at the Royal Australian College of Ophthalmologists.

•

A new Children's Eye Unit at the Great Ormond Street Hospital For Sick Children, London.

You can help further the work of the Foundation by making a donation or leaving a legacy. Every contribution, no matter how small, is received with gratitude. Please write for details to:

THE ULVERSCROFT FOUNDATION,
The Green, Bradgate Road, Anstey,
Leicester LE7 7FU, England.
Telephone: (0116) 236 4325

In Australia write to:

THE ULVERSCROFT FOUNDATION,
c/o The Royal Australian College of Ophthalmologists,
27, Commonwealth Street, Sydney,
N.S.W. 2010.

1

'Maria, love, there's a letter from the Isle of Man! It must be from Will. You see, he hasn't forgotten us after all!'

Maria gave the sheet she was washing a final, slightly vicious thump, before turning round to face her mother. Her attractive face was set in a frown.

'Well, it's certainly taken him enough time to answer. You wrote to him more than two months ago, didn't you?'

Jessie Oates sighed.

'You've got to remember that Will is a busy man, Maria. After all, he's got the farm to run. And anyway, men are different from women about writing letters. It takes them a lot of effort to actually sit down and get round to putting words on paper.'

Maria raised an eyebrow.

'Well, that's true enough, at least in

Will's case,' she answered. 'Why, he didn't even bother to send you a letter of condolence after you wrote and told him that Dad had died.'

'Don't be so bitter, Maria. After all, Jack wasn't his father. I think he rather resented me marrying again after Robert was drowned at sea. Will was very attached to his dad, just as you were to yours. In fact, I think that's why he took off and went to live on the island. There were too many memories here.'

'Possibly, although I'm sure Isobel and her father's farm were added incentives.'

'What a cynic you're becoming, Maria Oates! I'm sure their marriage is very happy, and they've got three children now. I must say, I'm really looking forward to seeing the little ones.'

'You're definitely thinking of going there, then?'

'Well of course. After all, we can hardly stay on here, with no money to pay the rent, now that you're not working.'

Jessie sank down on the wooden stool, and Maria thought, with a pang of guilt, that her mother was beginning to look much older. Her hair was quite grey and her face care-worn.

'Since there was that trouble with Mrs Macpherson, and they sent you off without a reference, things have gone from bad to worse,' Jessie continued, mournfully.

'But, Mother, what could I do?'

Maria shuddered at the unpleasant memory of John Macpherson's advances.

'I certainly didn't encourage her husband, if that's what you're thinking. He just grabbed hold of me and tried to kiss me, and Mrs Macpherson came into the room at that moment and jumped to all the wrong conclusions.'

'I'm not blaming you, love. It's not your fault that you're easily one of the prettiest girls in Ardrossan.'

Maria tried to suppress a giggle, and failed lamentably.

'Oh, Mother, you must be the only person who thinks so. Why, I'm almost five feet eight, and far too thin to be at all fashionable. My hair is quite mousy in colour and is so unruly. It's so thick and curly I just can't control it, no matter how I try! A beauty, I certainly am not! No, you should have let me take that job in Marson's factory.'

Jessie's mouth set in a grim line.

'I'm not having my only daughter working in a place like that, gutting fish all day. Oh no, Maria, I'd rather see us both starve than have you somewhere like that. And, perhaps you're not a conventional beauty, but you have a lovely face. There's such character in it, which is far more important to my way of thinking.'

Maria wiped her hands on the old grey towel, and embraced her mother.

'Sometimes, you're the most impossible old snob,' she exclaimed, affectionately. 'Come on, then, let's see what Will has to say, whether he's going to be our benefactor or not.'

The letter from Will Croft was impersonal and stilted. It did, however, offer a home to his mother and Maria, albeit grudgingly.

'Not exactly enthusiastic, is it?' Maria commented, without surprise.

Jessie, however, was disappointed in her son's letter.

'I would have expected a bit more warmth, but then, Will never did have much of a way with words?

Then she smiled, determined, as ever, to look on the bright side.

'Never mind, it'll all be right as rain once we get there, you'll see.'

Maria bit her lip.

'Then we really are going?' she asked again, a bit wistfully.

It wasn't that she had any great wish to stay in Ardrossan. Since her father had died in influenza, she had felt very lost and confused. The little, terraced house seemed to hold too many memories of happier times.

But although Will was fifteen years older than she was, and had left

Scotland ten years earlier, when Maria was only nine, she still remembered her half-brother as a cold, unfeeling man, who would cause trouble for her whenever an opportunity presented itself. No, Maria had no wish to have to accept charity from her brother Will.

Yet, what her mother had said was true — there was no way in which they were going to be able to keep the house on unless Maria found work. And, in Scotland, particularly here in Ardrossan, in 1896, finding work was no easy matter, particularly for a girl who had received some education, but had been dismissed without a reference.

No, all in all, the future looked bleak, and, like her mother, Maria knew that there was really no other option but to go to the Isle of Man, and Will's dubious charity.

With the decision made, they worked like Trojans, until the little two up, two down house was spick and span. Most of the furnishings belonged to Jessie, but she sold everything off at the salerooms. It was unlikely that Isobel would want her mother-in-law's furnishings cluttering the farmhouse.

With the money from the sale, they bought themselves some new dresses, two new bonnets, and a pair of smart, buttoned-up boots each, as well as a supply of undergarments and warm coats. At least they wouldn't be going to the island looking like paupers. That made Maria feel a bit better, and she couldn't help but notice that her mother looked younger, and more animated, than she'd seen her for weeks.

After they'd booked their passage, they still had almost forty pounds left. Of course, they would have to go carefully, but Maria was confident that she would soon be able to find a job as a lady's maid in one of the great houses on the island. Will's letter had hinted that his mother could help Isobel around the house, and that would at least pay for her keep.

Maria wasn't too happy about that. She was worried that they would use her mother as an unpaid servant. But perhaps she was worrying needlessly. After all, Will was Jessie's son. Surely he must have some affection for the woman who had given birth to him.

'I'm just going over to call on Clara and say goodbye to her, Mother. Do you want me to get anything while I'm out?' Maria called as they neared the hour of their departure.

'No, I don't think so, love. I bought some cheese and pickles yesterday, that should do for sandwiches to take on the boat, and I've made a stew which will do for our evening meal.

Her blue eyes, nothing like Maria's dark ones lit up with pleasure.

'Oh, love, I'm so excited! Do you know, this will be the first time I've ever been on a ship? In fact, I haven't been out of Scotland for close on two years.'

Maria smiled and hugged her mother lovingly before going out.

Jessie watched her go, a trim, smartly-dressed young woman who had all the local lads eyes turning to look at her as she walked down King Street, with never a look to right nor left. Maria was a proud girl, and she deserved to marry well, that she did, Jessie thought.

* * *

'I'll miss you, Maria, I really will,' Clara Wheeler exclaimed, hugging her friend to her. 'It was rotten of that Mrs Macpherson to treat you like she did. After all, everyone knows what that husband of hers is like!'

Maria smiled cynically.

'I've no doubt that she knows, too, but she's gentry. That makes all the difference, Clara.

'Yes, you're right there. Still, perhaps things will be better when you get to the Isle of Man. Why don't I get my mam to tell your fortune? As you know, she's the seventh daughter of a seventh daughter, and I'm sure she has the gift.'

Maria couldn't help but smile, caught

up in Clara's enthusiasm.

'Yes, I'd like that, if she will. I must admit I've always been a bit fascinated in things like that.'

'I know Ma would be glad to read the cards for you. She's upstairs doing some cleaning, but wait there a minute, and I'll go and fetch her.'

A moment or two later, Nellie Wheeler, came into the room, followed by Clara. Maria had never felt quite at ease with Nellie. She had a way of staring at you with her penetrating, dark eyes as if she could see right into your very soul.

Maria smiled at the older woman, but Nellie didn't smile back. Instead, she said, 'Clara tells me you want me to tell your fortune.'

'If you wouldn't mind, Mrs Wheeler. As Clara's probably told you, my mother and I are off to live on the Isle of Man, so it would be nice to have some idea how we'll get on there.'

'Looking forward to going to live

with your brother, are you?'

Maria gave a slightly nervous laugh. There was something about Mrs Wheeler that made her feel distinctly ill-at-ease.

'To tell you the truth, I don't know. I'll miss Clara, but living in King Street reminds me too much of my father. As to my brother . . .'

Maria hesitated slightly, wondering how to put it.

'Well, I was only a child when Will left,' she went on. 'I really don't remember him that well. After all, he's fifteen years older than I am.'

'And a mean-spirited fellow if ever there was one!' Nellie exclaimed, quite venomously. 'He's not like your mam, for there's no harm in Jessie. No he's a changeling, is that one!'

Maria was saved from answering by Clara coming back into the room carrying a pack of very old, worn-looking cards.

'There they are, Mam,' she said, putting the pack down on the table beside her mother then leaving.

When Nellie started shuffling the pack and turning cards over, Maria noticed that they were simply ordinary playing cards, although perhaps 'ordinary' wasn't quite the right word for them. They certainly looked as if they were at least one hundred years old, and didn't resemble any cards which she'd seen her father and his friends play with.

Nellie closed her eyes, and began to rock gently from side to side, while a strange moaning sound came from her slightly parted lips.

Then she suddenly opened her eyes, and grasped hold of two of the cards, holding them directly in front of her face, out of Maria's line of vision.

'Oh, my child, my child! It is as I feared. Sadness surrounds you, like a cloak of darkness.'

'What . . . what are you seeing?'

Maria's face was pale. Hadn't she known enough sadness with her father's untimely death? She watched as Nellie put the cards back on to the table, face down, and shuffled them with the others.

'I may have been mistaken. I've been feeling very tired lately.' She managed a wan smile. 'Arthritis creeping into these old bones of mine. Probably I just saw your past sadness, your dad's death. Yes, Maria, that was it. I saw him die of the influenza!'

Maria looked at her sadly.

'I know you're trying to be kind, Mrs Wheeler, to spare me the truth, but I'd rather know, really I would.'

Nellie Wheeler looked at Maria, her curious eyes almost opaque.

'Yes,' she said, at length. 'Yes, I think you would. Very well then, child. I saw death, the death of someone whom you care for very much. But it wasn't your dad's death, nor your mam's neither.'

'Then whose was it?' Maria asked, her voice scarcely more than a whisper.

Nellie Wheeler shook her head.

'I don't rightly know, Maria, but it was a man, a young man. I couldn't see his face too clearly, though, because there seemed to be a lot of smoke and fumes around.'

She screwed her face up in concentration.

'There's water, too, yes, I think there was water coming in from somewhere. But it was so indistinct, so shadowy. He was gasping for breath though, one hand raised and partially covering his face.'

Maria shivered at the picture which Nellie Wheeler had painted.

'And I know him, this man, who, presumably is going to die?' she asked.

'I don't think so, lass, I think he's someone whom you're going to meet and grow fond of,' Nellie whispered in reply.

'And there's nothing that I can do to save him? I mean, do you know what it is that's likely to kill him, so that I can try to stop him doing it?'

But Nellie Wheeler shook her head.

'No, Maria, lass, I'm afraid I don't. It was all too vague, almost like a dream that you can't fully remember. It could have been a fire. He seemed to be in a building of some sort, maybe his cottage. But I couldn't be sure. Anyway, it's my belief that it's very difficult to change fate, once it's been cast.'

'But don't you see anything good for me?' Maria asked, almost imploringly.

Nellie sighed, picked up the cards once more and shuffled through them, before fanning them out before Maria.

'Shut your eyes and pick three of these and I'll try to read them for you.'

Maria, her heart beating erratically, did as Nellie asked.

'Now give them to me, and when you've done so, you can open your eyes.'

Maria handed them to Nellie, opened her eyes, and said, questioningly, 'Well?'

Nellie shrugged.

'They're a mixed bag, really. I can see you're going on a journey soon, well, we know that to be true, don't we? And then there's the Queen of Hearts — a fair woman. Do you know any fair women?'

'I think, Isobel, my brother's wife is fair,' Maria replied, a trifle uncertainly.

It was years since she'd seen Isobel, and then only for the month that she'd spent in Ardrossan visiting some cousins of her mother's.

Nellie Wheeler shook her head.

'Not a happy one, that. Regretting her marriage to your brother, I shouldn't doubt. And not well, neither, although she'll live a good few years longer yet. And the third card . . .' She hesitated. 'It signifies hardship, lack of money. Is that farm of your brother's doing well?'

'I was always led to think so,' Maria replied. 'In fact, I always felt that it was a desire to get his hands on the farm that led my brother to marry Isobel in the first place, although Mum accuses me of being a cynic for saying things like that.'

'Sounds in keeping with his character,

if you ask me,' Nellie said. 'Anyway, I would say that the farm has probably been losing money of late. Tell your mother to take care. She may well find herself in the rôle of an unpaid servant if she's not careful.'

'You know, Mrs Wheeler, that's something which I've been worrying about myself,' Maria replied. In his letter, Will said that Mum could help Isobel around the house.'

Nellie nodded.

'Well, tell her to watch out. She's not a young woman any more, and wants to be taking things a bit easier these days.'

As she spoke, she put the cards back in the pack.

'Well, that's it, girl.'

* * *

Maria and her mother set sail for Douglas, on the Isle of Man, the following day.

It was a very breezy day for mid-May,

and Maria felt her stomach begin to churn alarmingly when she saw the impressive steam packet vessel bobbing up and down in the comparative shelter of the harbour.

'If it's like this here, what's it going to be like when we actually get out on the open sea?' she said, turning to her mother.

'Oh don't be so chicken-hearted, Maria!' Jessie admonished, gaily. 'After all, it's not a very long trip. It only takes seven hours when all's said and done.'

'Seven hours!' Maria exclaimed, in a horrified tone, as one of the seamen courteously carried their larger suitcase on board for them. Maria carried the smaller one.

'Don't worry, love,' he said, reassuringly. 'I've been on a lot worse journeys than you're likely to have today, I can tell you! It'll be a bit choppy, like, but once you find your sea legs, you'll be all right, and I reckon this wind is going to die down quite a bit in the next few hours anyway.'

Maria smiled up at the tall, suntanned man. He had the most attractive blue eyes that she'd ever seen, she thought, conscious of an unfamiliar fluttering in her stomach.

Nerves, she thought to herself. Yes, nerves, that's what it is. Yet there was something very appealing about the man who was smiling back down at her.

When they were on deck, the young seaman took Maria's small case from her.

'I'm sorry, lass. I didn't notice that you were carrying a case as well, or I'd have carried it up the gang plank for you.'

Maria laughed.

'Really, there's no need for you to carry it at all. It's not very heavy. That's probably why you didn't notice that I had it in the first place.'

'Nevertheless, it's not for a lady like yourself to have to carry her own luggage around.'

He turned to Jessie then.

'I hope you don't think me impertinent, ma'am, but are you two ladies travelling alone?'

'We are,' Jessie replied. 'I'm recently widowed and my son, who farms on the Isle of Man, has invited my daughter and myself to come there and join him.'

'Oh, right, I see. I wonder if I know him. After all, the island's not such a big place. What part of the island is his farm in?' As he spoke, he began moving off at an unhurried pace, Jessie and Maria walking beside him, Jessie nearest.

'It's near a place called Maughold.'

'Actually, I'm not too far from there myself. I live just outside Laxey, on the road which leads down to Ramsey. Your Maughold is a turning off that road.'

He stopped, and put the two cases down on the deck outside a room which proclaimed, 'Ladies Lounge.' He smiled ruefully.

'I'd take them inside for you, but it would be more than my life was worth. Mrs Christian, who's in charge of the lounge, is a veritable dragon.'

He held out his hand to Jessie, and she extended her own, which he shook warmly.

'It's been my pleasure meeting you, ma'am, and your beautiful daughter. I assume this is your daughter.'

'Yes, she's my daughter, Maria Oates, and I'm Jessica Oates. And you, young man, what's your name?'

The young seaman smiled, blue eyes twinkling.

'I'm Robert Cregeen, although everyone calls me Rob. Would you mind telling me, ma'am, where exactly you'll be living in Maughold? With your permission, I could perhaps call on you and show you both something of the island. My dad has a pony and trap which I know he'd let me borrow.'

'Well, I'm sure Maria would appreciate having a friend on the island,' Jessie replied, looking pointedly at her daughter, who couldn't quite prevent a telling blush from staining her cheeks. 'All right then, Mr Cregeen, that seems a very kind offer, although I'm not quite fool enough to think it's me to whom you wish to show your island.'

She held up her hand, as Robert opened his mouth to protests.

'No, I quite understand. I was young once myself, you know! If you wish to call on us, we will be staying at Cushag farm, the home of Mr and Mrs William Croft. Maria, of course, may not be there all that long, since she intends to seek a position as a lady's maid.'

Jessie paused, suddenly becoming aware that underneath his tan, Robert Cregeen had turned quite pale.

'What is it, young man? What's the matter?' she asked, suddenly anxious. 'Aren't you feeling well?'

Rob forced himself to smile.

'Nothing to fret about, ma'am,' he assured her, with a confidence he was far from feeling. 'Someone just walked over my grave, as they say.'

But deep inside, he was feeling very disturbed. The lovely Maria, the most attractive girl he had ever laid eyes on, was obviously the sister of the hateful and hated Will Croft. Rob needed no reminding of how that very man had laid a man trap, even though they had been outlawed countless years before, and caught his young brother Johnnie in it.

Young Johnnie was alive, thanks only to Isobel Croft, but his legs were ruined. He could hobble around on crutches, but he'd never walk again!

2

Rob Cregeen pulled himself together with an effort. Of course, there was no proof that Croft had laid the trap, although, knowing his vicious nature, Rob didn't doubt for one moment that he had.

Croft had sworn in court that he knew nothing about it. The magistrate, incompetent fool that he was, had believed him. Or had he? Rob didn't really know.

It might have been that old Benjamin Kerruish, Isobel's father, had used his considerable wealth to influence the matter. Whatever it was, Will Croft walked off a free man, the magistrate referring to Johnnie's loss of the use of his legs as a most unfortunate incident, and saying that it probably wouldn't have been much worse if Johnnie had been caught in a legal gin trap.

Rob supposed it was true. Gin traps had savage pronged teeth, too, but that didn't get away from the fact that it might have been fatal if Isobel Croft hadn't been walking in the small woods which belonged to the farm. She had heard Johnnie's agonised cries for help, and, somehow, with a strength which belied her slight form, managed to prise open the trap and free the ten-year-old.

'You're looking very thoughtful, Mr Cregeen,' Maria said, breaking into his troubled thoughts. 'We haven't said or done anything to offend you, I hope?'

Rob shook his head, a lock of dark brown hair falling over his forehead. He shook it away impatiently.

'No, no, of course you haven't, Miss Maria. I was just thinking that I'd better be getting back to work. I'll come back here just before the ship is due to dock, so keep a look-out for me. Then I can carry your cases off for you.'

He inclined his head.

'Until later, ladies, and I hope that you have a comfortable journey.'

'Something upset him,' Maria said, abruptly, once her mother and herself were seated in the spacious, comfortable ladies' lounge. 'What do you think it could have been? It was after you told him where we'll be staying, wasn't it? After you told him that Will was your son. Oh, Mum, do you think Will's done something to him at some time?'

'Oh, nonsense, Maria! What a vivid imagination you've got. I'm sure it's nothing of the sort.'

But, as she spoke, her face was anxious. She knew that Will had always possessed a very bad temper, possibly inherited from her first husband's father, a drunkard who had knocked his family about. Will had been more subtle than that, but he was one to hold a grudge, and if he imagined that he'd been slighted in any way, the unfortunate victim would always pay for it. But Jessie hadn't seen Will for years. Marriage and children would surely have mellowed him. Maria remained unconvinced, however.

'I know Will's done something, and I won't rest until I find out what it is!' she exclaimed, her face set in determined lines.

She passed a hand over her forehead, and it came away sticky with perspiration.

'Goodness, but it's hot in here. If you don't mind, Mother, I think I'll go back up on deck and watch the ship setting off. It's due to leave in just over five minutes.'

'I'll come with you,' Jessie said quickly.

She didn't want Maria wandering around on deck on her own. Goodness knows whom she might meet. Robert Cregeen had seemed a decent enough fellow, but the boat seemed quite crowded. There could well be undesirables on board.

'We'll leave our baggage here to reserve our places,' she said, firmly.

'Anyway, I'd like to see my homeland vanishing in the distance. After all, it could well be a very long time before I see Scotland again.'

She shrugged, and Maria saw that her mother's eyes were glistening with unshed tears. Maria linked her arm through her mother's and they made their way back up on deck.

'We didn't have to leave, you know,' Maria was saying. 'I could have found another job, even if it was in a different part of Scotland. I thought you wanted to come. You seemed so excited about it all.'

'Take no notice of me. I'll be fine once we're actually on our way. It's just the leaving after so many years that's hard. But I know it's for the best. We need a change of scenery after your father's death, and there'll be more opportunities for you.'

They went out on deck and stood by the railings, looking at the quayside, the wind pulling at their bonnets, so that they had to secure them more tightly under their chins. A minute or two later, there was a loud hooting sound, and the stately vessel made her way out of the harbour and into the open sea.

Jessie stepped back from the railings as spray churned upwards and caught her in the face.

'Well, I don't know about you, young lady, but in my opinion it's getting a bit rough to be standing around up here. I think we should go back downstairs and get our heads down.'

Maria was actually feeling better in the fresh air than the stuffy lounge, but she decided she was being selfish, so, taking her mother's arm, she led the older woman back downstairs.

Within a few minutes, Jessie was lying on one of the couches, a pillow behind her head, and a thick rug covering her. Maria guessed that she was dozing, and took a novel out of her bag and began reading. But the words seemed to dance before her eyes, due to the ship's increasing movement, and she quickly put it to one side.

'You'd be better following the other lady's example. Your mother, I take it?'

Maria nodded at the tall, well-built woman. Obviously, she must be 'the dragon', Mrs Christian, whom Rob had mentioned.

'Get your head down,' the imposing figure advised. 'That way you'll probably manage to drop off to sleep, and the worst part of the journey will be over without you knowing anything about it.'

'Yes, I will, thank you,' Maria replied obediently, aware that she was feeling a bit dizzy.

She had to admit that it was better lying down, and after several minutes she managed to nod off.

When she woke up, she saw that it was almost half past four. Well, at least she'd slept through the best part of the journey. Only another couple of hours left. She was feeling very thirsty, though, and decided to go and get a drink.

One glance at her mother told her that Jessie was still sleeping peacefully, so Maria decided not to disturb her, but to fetch a couple of cups of tea, as she felt sure that Jessie would welcome one.

The sea had calmed down considerably, so that it was quite easy to make her way to the buffet. She bought a pot of tea and was just moving away from the buffet, balancing the tray when she almost literally bumped into Rob. His handsome face broke into a smile when he saw her.

'So, how is the journey going? I hope you've managed to enjoy it even if it has been a bit on the rough side. Are you still downstairs in the ladies' lounge?'

He took the tea from her and moved towards the staircase.

'Yes, my mother's still asleep, and I have to confess that I've slept most of the journey. Mrs Christian advised me to.'

Maria smiled up at him, thinking that it was a change for her to find a man who was actually taller than her five feet eight.

'You said that she was a dragon, but actually, she was quite nice.'

'She's not too bad with the female passengers. It's us male crew members whom she gives a hard time to. Anyway, on this occasion, she was right, you were just as well sleeping through it. Mind you, we've made good time. I reckon we should be docking in Douglas soon after six.'

'I won't be sorry,' Maria admitted, as she followed Rob. 'I don't think sailing is my forte.'

'Is this the first time that you've been on a ship?'

'Yes, it is, actually.'

'Well, you've had a tough enough initiation. Sometimes the sea is like a mill pond. I get a discount with working for the company. You'll have to let me take you on a day trip to Dublin some time. I'm sure you'd enjoy it.'

To her embarrassment, Maria found that she was blushing, and only hoped that Rob didn't notice.

'That would be nice,' she murmured. 'Mind you, I don't know what time I'll have. I'll need to look for a job as soon as possible.'

By this time, they had reached the outside of the lounge, where they both paused.

'Aye, well, I'll not pretend that I wouldn't be happier seeing you out of Croft's household,' Rob admitted. 'Your mother said that you're a lady's maid?'

Maria nodded.

'But why would you want me away from my brother's house?' she asked, seeing her opportunity to find out why Robert Cregeen disliked Will.

Robert Cregeen's lips tightened.

'Let's just say that your brother is not one of my favourite people.'

As he spoke, he handed Maria the drinks.

'You'd best take these in there now, lass, else it'll be going cold. I'll be back for you just before we dock.'

Then, before Maria could question him further, he was gone, and she was left holding the tray, a puzzled expression on her face as she looked after him.

Shaking her head, she balanced the tea in one hand and opened the door of the lounge, making her way past several recumbent bodies before she reached the cushioned sofa where Jessie was now sitting up.

'Maria, love! I was wondering where on earth you'd got to. Ah, but I see you've been out fetching tea. How thoughtful of you! At the moment, there's nothing I feel like more than a nice refreshing cup of tea.'

Maria smiled.

'You slept well, Mother! Well, I suppose we both did, really. I only woke up a few minutes before you.'

She put the tray down on the table and poured the tea from the pewter teapot into the two cups, handing one to her mother.

'I met Rob while I was getting the tea. He says that we'll be arriving in Douglas early, around six o'clock.'

Jessie raised her eyebrows.

'Oh, you did, did you? Just by accident, was it?'

Maria looked exasperated.

'Well, of course it was! After all, I told you that I only woke up shortly before you did.'

Jessie leaned over and patted her hand.

'Yes, I'm sure it was, love. I'm afraid you'll just have to forgive an over-protective mother.'

'I'm nineteen, mother. At my age you were married and had Will.' Her face tightened. 'Rob doesn't like Will. He admitted that to me, but he wouldn't say why.'

Jessie sighed.

'Why can't life ever go smoothly?'

she murmured, almost to herself. 'Rob seems a nice enough lad, but then, we don't really know him, do we? Whereas your brother . . . '

Her voice trailed off aimlessly.

'My half-brother,' Maria corrected.

'Yes, dear, I know, but he's also my son!' Jessie exclaimed, her voice distressed.

'Yes, and I'm sure that things are just getting blown out of all proportion,' Maria said quickly, anxious to reassure her mother. 'I can't pretend to being overly fond of Will when I was a child, but I'm sure everything is going to be very different now. After all, he didn't have to offer us a home. If he hadn't cared about us, then he wouldn't have done so, would he?'

'He has a strong sense of duty, and that's a good quality,' Jessie replied, conscious of the fact that the words had a hollow ring about them.

She decided that it might be wise to change the subject.

'Rob might well be able to help

you find a position as a lady's maid, mightn't he? After all, he must know which families would be likely to be looking for help.'

'I wasn't talking to him for long,' Maria admitted. 'But, yes, I'm sure that he will know of families I could approach. Anyway, he's coming back here to help us with our luggage just before the ship docks. Perhaps I could ask him then.'

'Yes, dear, that's probably a good idea, although he did say that he'd call on us and take us out to show us something of the island.'

'That was before he knew where we would be staying, Mother, before he knew that I'm Will's sister, and you're his mother!'

Rob began waiting outside the ladies' lounge shortly after half past five. Much too early, he knew, but he wanted to see Maria. He was lucky. At precisely twenty to six, Maria came out of the lounge.

'Well, hello again,' he said, trying to

sound as though he had been passing by chance.

Maria seemed startled to see him there.

'Rob, what are you doing here already?'

'I took a chance, hoping I would see you. I wanted to speak to you.'

Maria couldn't help but be flattered, and she answered, truthfully.

'And I came out of the lounge, because I hoped that you might be here!'

They both laughed, before Rob continued.

'I think I could definitely get to be very fond of you, Maria Oates, but I just can't hide my intense dislike of your brother.'

'He's only my half-brother,' Maria replied, tremulously.

Rob's face lightened.

'He is? Why didn't you say so before!'

'Well, for one thing, you didn't give me much of a chance. Anyway, does it really make that much difference? After all, we're still the same flesh and blood.'

'You're nothing like him, neither is your mother. Obviously, I don't know her well, but she seems to be a very pleasant sort of person.'

'She's the best mother anyone could have,' Maria replied, sincerely.

'Yes, I'm sure she is.' He sighed. 'Ah, well, it's no use letting Will Croft spoil our chance of happiness, is it? He's already caused quite enough trouble.'

Maria put her hand on his sleeve, and looked up at him anxiously.

'Just what has Will done to you?' she inquired.

'It's in the past, and best forgotten,' Rob replied, shaking his head.

'But I want to know,' Maria insisted.

Rob hesitated. Maria saw that he was wavering, and seized her opportunity.

'I'm warning you, Robert Cregeen. If you don't tell me, I won't see you again.'

He smiled.

'A wilful little minx, aren't you? Very well then.'

And he told her what had happened to his young brother Johnnie, and as he spoke, Maria's face paled.

'And you're sure that he set the trap?' she asked in a voice scarcely more than a whisper.

'I can't be sure, but there were a lot of poachers around at that time, and the Croft's wood was a place they tended to head for. Young Johnnie wasn't poaching. He was looking for his dog, which had gone missing earlier that morning.'

Rob's mouth tightened.

'I found Skipper later that day. He'd been shot. Will Croft maintained he was chasing his sheep, but it wasn't true. Skipper was as gentle as a lamb himself.'

'I can see why you must hate him.' Maria sighed deeply. 'I honestly feel ashamed that I'm related to him.'

Rob put an arm round her shoulders,

and briefly hugged her to him.

'It's not your fault, and I may well be mistaken about Johnnie.'

But neither he nor Maria believed that he was . . .

When Maria and Jessie got off the ship, with Rob carrying their cases, Douglas was bathed in sunshine, the three-mile long promenade bustling with people.

'Well, it certainly looks a grand place,' Jessie exclaimed, looking about her. 'And so busy! Why, I was imagining somewhere quite quiet.'

Rob smiled.

'You must remember, Mrs Oates, that we're still in the summer season. September can be one of our busiest months. Right then, how are you getting to the Croft's farm? Is someone coming to meet you?'

Jessie shook her head a bit ruefully.

'No. Will's too busy on the farm for such niceties, I'm afraid. But Isobel did give us instructions how to get there.'

She reached into her bag and took

out a sheet of paper.

'She says that probably the best thing for us to do is take a horse tram or omnibus to the terminus stop where the electric trams go from. Then we can take that to the tram stop in Maughold. Isobel will wait for us there with the pony and trap.'

'I'll see you safely on to the horse-tram,' Rob said, 'and then I must return to the ship. I'll be staying on board her tonight ready for the morning trip.'

'You must work long hours,' Maria remarked, as they made their way to a waiting horse tram.

'In the summer, things are very hectic, but it slows down a lot in winter. In summer we'd be glad of a day off, and in the winter we'd be glad of a day on. We get paid for the hours we put in, you see. Still, that's life, and I enjoy being out at sea.'

He turned and smiled at Maria then spoke to Jessie.

'I'm due a day off on Thursday, so if it's all right by you, ma'am, I'll call on you both then and show you something of the island. That gives you a couple of days to settle in.'

'We'll both look forward to seeing you, Mr Cregeen, and thank you for carrying our luggage,' Jessie said, smiling at Rob as he hoisted their cases on to the horse tram.

'Goodbye, Rob, until Thursday,' Maria murmured, taking her seat on the tram.

Rob stood watching as the tram pulled away, returning Jessie and Maria's wave. Then he turned away, and headed back to the pier.

When Jessie and Maria eventually ended their journey from Douglas, Isobel was waiting at the little station at Maughold.

Maria doubted very much that she would have recognised her sister-in-law, but she was the only one there. She looked very different from the carefree, young girl who had come to Scotland ten years before.

'Isobel, dear, how lovely to see you!'

Jessie exclaimed, as Isobel climbed down from the trap and embraced her mother-in-law.

'It's good to see you, too, Mrs Oates,' Isobel said, and Maria was surprised to see that her clear, blue eyes were misty with tears.

'You mustn't call me Mrs Oates, child,' Jessie admonished gently. 'Please, call me mother, even if we haven't seen much of one another.'

Then she pushed Maria forward.

'This is Maria. I bet you'll find her looking rather different from when you saw her last.'

'I certainly do!' Isobel exclaimed, embracing her sister-in-law. 'Why, Maria, you were only a child when I last saw you, and now you're a beautiful young lady. I'm sure Will will be proud that he's got such a lovely sister.'

But to Maria, her voice sounded uncertain.

'Maybe so,' Maria replied. 'How is Will, by the way?'

'Oh, very busy with the farm,

otherwise I'm sure he'd have been here to meet you himself. But let's get on our way. It's starting to get a bit cold. Here, let me help you up into the trap.'

She took Jessie's arm and helped her up, Maria following. 'We'd best be on our way, you'll no doubt be anxious to see Will.'

'I'm looking forward to seeing him and the children. How old are they now, Isobel? I'm afraid I quite lose track of time.'

'Young William is nine, Jane is seven and Michael's just turned five. They'll be in bed by the time we get back, as we tend to go to bed early as we have to be up soon after dawn.'

'Yes, you must have a lot to do. Well, I'll certainly help you all I can, and Maria will, too, that is, until she can find a job. Is there much work available, Isobel? She's worked as a lady's maid.'

Isobel bit her lip.

'Yes, I know, you told me in one

of your letters, and I told Will. When he knew that you'd both definitely be coming to live with us here, he made enquiries and found out that the Pennington's, the major shareholders in the Laxey mines, need a lady's maid for Mrs Pennington. They live in a big house just outside the village.'

She looked at Maria apologetically.

'I know it's very little warning, but Will's arranged for you to go there for an interview at ten o'clock tomorrow morning. That's how Will is, I'm afraid. Once he gets an idea in his head, he acts on it immediately.'

'That was very thoughtful of him,' Jessie said quickly.

But she saw the look of consternation on Maria's face, and rightly interpreted that her daughter was temporarily lost for words. Thoughtful Will was not, despite what she'd said just then. More than likely he just wanted Maria out of the house as quickly as possible so that he wouldn't have to keep her. Looking at her daughter, Jessie was fully aware that that was what Maria thought, too.

'What sort of a family are they, these Penningtons?' Maria asked, her voice slightly tremulous at the certain knowledge that her half-brother didn't want her.

'What can I say?' Isobel began lamely. 'Our sort of people don't really mix with the gentry. Mr Pennington is thought to be a hard, haughty sort of man, but from what I've seen of his wife, she looks an agreeable enough kind of person. Very smartly dressed, and attractive.

'Then there's a son and two daughters. You won't see much of the elder girl, Caroline, as she's married to a colonel and lives on the mainland. The younger one, Felicity, lives at home, and from what I've heard, she's a spoiled madam. Mind you, that could just be servants' gossip.

'And then there's the son, Daniel. He's recently finished at Cambridge, and come back to live at home until he decides what he wants to do. His father, of course, wants him to go into the family business, the mines, on the managerial side. But rumour has it that young Daniel and his father don't always get along too well. Mr Pennington is of the old school, and I hear that he considers most of Daniel's ideas of improved conditions for the men are revolutionary, and guaranteed to lead to strikes and insurrections.'

'And this is the household that Will is thinking of for Maria?' Jessie's voice was horrified. 'Why, I swear if I'd known about this before, I'd have been very tempted to stay in Scotland. Just wait until I see Will!'

Isobel looked back at her imploringly. 'Oh, please don't say anything to him, Mother, because then he'll know that I've been talking, and he'll be very angry, and probably he'll h . . . ' She broke off.

'Were you going to say that Will hits you, Isobel?' Jessie asked quietly.

'Yes! No! Well, only occasionally,'

Isobel murmured, her voice full of shame.

'I'll have to speak to him,' Jessie whispered but Isobel had heard.

'Oh, no, please don't!' she begged. 'It'll only make things much worse. Will has a very fiery temper, but I'm sure he doesn't mean any real harm.'

Jessie's lips tightened.

'Well, we'll see,' she said, and with that, Isobel had to be content, although Maria noticed that her hands holding the reins were shaking.

When they arrived at the farm and went indoors, Will Croft was, unknown to them, sitting in the large, old-fashioned farmhouse kitchen, eating the cold supper which Isobel had prepared for him before she left.

'Will, where are you?' Isobel called from the hallway. 'You're mother and sister are here.'

'In the kitchen having my supper, woman! Where do you think?' he called out in his gruff voice.

Maria shook her head, and mouthed

to her mother, 'I can see he hasn't changed!'

Isobel smiled nervously.

'It's this way. Come on in, and you can have a chat with him while I fetch you something to eat. I've made some sandwiches and cakes. Will that be all right, or would you rather have something warm?'

'No, that'll be fine, thank you, Isobel,' Jessie answered.

Will didn't even bother to look up as they entered the room, until Isobel coughed to draw his attention. A sardonic smile played about his thin, cruel lips. 'Why Mother, it's good to see you. Do sit down. And this must be Maria.'

He shook his head, his untidy brown hair falling forward over his slightly fleshy face.

'I must say, I wouldn't have recognised her, although she's the image of Jack Oates, isn't she, Mother?'

Jessie's heart sank. If Will could see a likeness to Jack in Maria, he would be likely to be more antagonistic towards her.

'Personally, I like to think she favours me,' she said, sitting down beside Will. Maria sat on her other side, while Isobel stood uncertainly in the doorway. Will threw back his head and laughed unpleasantly.

'Well, you might like to think so, Mother, but I assure you, you're only deluding yourself. She's an Oates!'

Then he turned to Isobel.

'Well, don't just stand there! Go and fetch them some food, and make a fresh pot of tea. And be quick about it!'

Isobel hurried into the pantry without a word. Jessie shook her head.

'Do you always speak to Isobel like that?' she asked once her daughter-in-law was out of earshot.

'On a good day, yes. And you must admit, Mother, that today is just that. After all, it must be all of ten years since I've had the pleasure of seeing you both.'

'It was very kind of you to offer us a home,' Jessie said, striving to be affable, although Maria thought that her mother already looked strained.

'I'm offering you a home because you're my mother,' Will replied. 'But I don't see why I should keep that great lump of a girl!'

He nodded disparagingly at Maria.

'So you'll be pleased to hear that I've arranged an interview for her at Pennington Hall tomorrow morning.'

He went on to tell them about it, with several more embellishments than Isobel had. Jessie heard him out in silence, although two spots of colour appeared in her cheeks, and her hands were trembling with rage.

'If Marie doesn't like the Penningtons, she's not staying there,' she said flatly. 'We've some money left, and we can always find lodgings elsewhere and look for work. We don't have to be beholden to you if that's your attitude.'

'What gratitude!' Will exclaimed, with a nasty smile, as Isobel brought in a tray piled high with sandwiches and cakes, and a huge earthenware teapot. 'Put those down and then do join us, dear. Then you can see for yourself just how much my mother and sister appreciate my efforts on their behalf.'

'Your mother and sister will be tired after their journey, Will. Perhaps it would be best if you and I take tea in the parlour and leave them to have their supper in peace.'

Will immediately rounded on his wife.

'Are you telling me what to do, Isobel?'

It was Jessie who answered, speaking directly to Isobel.

'You're right, my dear. We are tired. Perhaps you wouldn't mind if we don't have supper and go straight to bed. I'm sure things will seem much clearer in the morning.'

'But, of course. I'll show you to your rooms. They're next to one another.'

And with that, Jessie and Maria followed Isobel out of the room, Will staring after them, open-mouthed. He had the distinct feeling that they'd got the better of him, but, at that moment, he couldn't think what to do about it.

That night Maria found it almost impossible to get off to sleep. Her mind was in a turmoil.

She was sure she wasn't going to like the Penningtons, but she was equally sure that she would take their job, if they offered it to her, that was. What alternative did she have? With her out of the way, Will would probably be tolerable to Jessie, and she couldn't drag her poor mother into lodgings while she traipsed about looking for work.

They just didn't have that sort of money, and Will wouldn't take Jessie back if she left, of that Maria was sure. Somehow, whatever her personal feelings, she would just have to make sure that Mrs Pennington gave her the job.

3

Maria was up earlier than she needed to be the following morning. She was so tensed up at the prospect of her forthcoming interview at Pennington Hall that she found it impossible to settle, and knew that she would have to get up and busy herself.

It was only six thirty as she made her way silently downstairs to the kitchen. But she had temporarily forgotten that this was a farmhouse, and that the Crofts were very early risers.

'Good morning, Maria.'

Isobel, already elbow deep in the pastry she was making, smiled at her.

'I must say that I didn't expect to see you up and about so soon. The bed was comfortable, I hope?'

Maria nodded but she was temporarily disconcerted, particularly as Will was sitting at the table, tucking into a hearty, cooked breakfast. He hadn't even lifted his head as she entered the kitchen.

Isobel turned to Maria, and, wiping her arms and hands with a damp cloth, said, 'But I expect you'd like some warm water for washing. I'll just heat a kettle for you.'

By the time Maria arrived back in the kitchen, her mother and three young relatives were already there, all tucking into hearty breakfasts. The youngest one, a tousled-haired fellow with a cheeky grin, looked up as Maria entered.

'You must be our Auntie Maria. You don't look much like Pa,' he said.

'Yes, I'm your Auntie Maria, but I'm your daddy's half-sister, which is probably why I look quite different.'

'What's a half-sister?' young Michael asked.

Maria opened her mouth to reply, but was beaten to it by William.

'It means that Pa and Aunt Maria had the same mother, but different father, stupid!'

'I am not stupid!' Michael's voice was shrill with indignation, as he picked up a piece of bread and threw it at his elder brother.

Jessie shook her head.

'Oh, dear, even at five years old I see young Michael has traces of his father's temper!'

'William, don't you dare throw a piece back at him!'

Isobel admonished her elder son, who had the grace to look a bit shame-faced, as he put the piece of bread which he'd been about to throw back on the plate.

As she spoke, she opened the oven door, and took out a plate of bacon and eggs, which she put on the table.

'That's for you, Maria. Sit down there next to Jane. I haven't introduced you to my daughter, have I?'

Maria smiled at the pretty, delicate-looking, young girl.

'Hello, Jane, it's lovely to meet you at last.'

Jane looked up at her shyly.

'You've got a beautiful gown on, Aunt Maria. That sort of pink colour is really nice. It makes you look, well, sort of foreign.'

'My word, Jane,' Isobel said suddenly, 'that's a lot of chat coming from you. Obviously you've made a hit there, Maria!'

The atmosphere was light and bantering, and Maria thought how different it would be if her half-brother had still been there. Involuntarily, she shivered. To her surprise, Jane noticed.

'Are you cold, Aunt Maria? If you are, I can stoke the fire up a bit. We don't normally have a fire in September, but after all the nice weather we've had, it's quite chilly this morning.'

Maria patted her hand.

'No, dear, I'm fine. I was just thinking about something, that's all.'

The child's eyes widened.

'Something not nice? Like Pa?' she asked.

Maria didn't know what to say. She was saddened that the little girl should feel like that about Will, and yet, at the same time, who could blame her? Fortunately, she was saved from answering by Isobel clapping her hands and telling the children it was time they set off for school. That sent them scampering off.

Jessie looked slightly stunned as the youngsters slammed the door.

'Goodness me, but you've got a handful there, Isobel. I do declare, I'd quite forgotten just how noisy children can be.'

Isobel smiled.

'Oh, they were showing off a bit today. They didn't upset you, did they? Actually, Jane's very quiet. I was amazed that she talked to Maria as much as she did.'

Jessie shook her head.

'No, they didn't upset me, Isobel. They're bonny children and you must be really proud of them. It's just that I'm getting to be an old woman, but, hopefully, they'll help me to get a more youthful outlook.'

She turned to Maria.

'You're looking very smart, love. You're not still nervous about the interview, are you?'

Maria shook her head.

'No,' she fibbed. 'I was just feeling tired last night, that's all. Things always seem a bit worse when you're tired.'

Jessie didn't look totally convinced, but she let the subject drop, wisely.

'I'll come with you, Maria,' Isobel said suddenly. 'Just give me a chance to get these cakes in the oven, and I'll take you there in the trap.'

'Oh, no, there's no need for that, Isobel. There must be a tram going there. They live just outside Laxey, don't they?'

'Yes, it's a great big house just before the Laxey station. It's got a very imposing entrance, with two pillars done in the shape of stone lions.'

Maria smiled.

'Well, then, I won't be able to miss

it, will I? No, Isobel, you carry on with your work. You seem to have more than enough to do.'

'Well, if you're sure, but I'll take you to the tram stop. There's a tram at nine twenty, that'll get you there in plenty of time.'

That decided, Jessie helped Isobel to finish the baking. Maria passed the remaining hour or so combing out her long hair, and, fixing it into a neat chignon, it looked very elegant under her smart, little hat.

She and Isobel then made their way to the main road.

'There's the electric tram,' Isobel said when they reached the little station. 'You buy your ticket from that little hut. Now, are you sure you'll be all right?'

'Yes, Isobel, very sure. I'm going to get this job, you know. Just you wait and see!'

The journey didn't take long, and Maria was soon alighting at Laxey station. She took the precaution of asking the station master where the Pennington's residence was, and the man, a cheerful-looking fellow, told her that it was only about five minutes walk away, and pointed her in the right direction.

Maria's new-found confidence faltered a little, however, when she actually saw the imposing entrance to Pennington Hall. Isobel had been right about the lions. They were perched on two pillars, and looked wild and exotic, almost as if they were ready to spring off.

She struggled a little with the wrought-iron gates, but finally managed to get the bolt to slip back. Once inside, she began to walk down the long, gravelled driveway, lined with tall, unyielding trees.

The drive must have stretched for the best part of a quarter of a mile, and Maria's feet, encased in her shiny, new, laced-up bootees, were starting to feel quite sore when she finally reached Pennington Hall.

She stopped, drawing in her breath,

as she took in the beauty of the elegant, eighteenth-century building. She had known that the Penningtons were wealthy, but to own and maintain a place like this, they must be extremely so.

She mustn't allow herself to become over-awed, she told herself, crossly, as she stepped forward, and lifted the heavy, brass door knocker.

After what was probably less than a couple of minutes, but felt, to Maria, at least three times longer, the door was opened by a supercilious-looking man, immaculate in a dark, formal suit.

'Yes?' he said, looking down his nose at her. 'You have some business at the hall?'

'Yes, I do,' Maria replied, annoyed to find that her voice held a slight tremble. 'I have an appointment to see Mrs Pennington at ten o'clock.'

When he didn't answer right away, she hurried on.

'You will be Mr Pennington, I expect.'

She held out her hand.

'My name is Maria Oates, and I'm very pleased to make your acquaintance.'

If possible, the man's expression became even frostier.

'My dear young lady, I am John Bates, the butler here. Mr Marcus Pennington is not in the habit of answering his own door!'

Maria blushed. Oh, how could she have been so stupid! It was nerves, that's what it was. She wasn't thinking clearly. Of course people like the Penningtons would have a butler.

'I take it that Mrs Rachel Pennington is interviewing you for some kind of employment, in which case, it is customary to use the tradespeople's and servants' entrance. You'll find that at the right-hand side of the house.

He made to shut the door in Maria's face, but the door was grasped suddenly by another hand, and pulled open, to reveal a strikingly handsome young man, around twenty-five or so.

'I say there, Bates, what's going on

here? Aren't you even going to let the young lady in?'

'The lady,' he said with a disparaging emphasis on the latter word, 'has come about employment, and I was just telling her that it's customary for a prospective employee to use the servants' entrance.'

'Oh, what pompous rubbish! Go back in, Bates. I'll handle this.'

Bates bowed stiffly.

'Very well, Mr Daniel.'

From his tone of voice, it was quite obvious that he didn't approve, Maria thought, but her thoughts didn't dwell on Bates as she found herself staring at the handsome stranger.

So this was Daniel Pennington — the Penningtons' only son. Well, he was certainly handsome enough, and, more important, he seemed kind, too.

'Don't let the old fellow get you down. He used to work in a duke's household, and I'm afraid he still tends to live in the past. We try to keep things a little more informal.'

He smiled ironically.

'Or at least I do, although I'm afraid father's still inclined to be stuck in the old school.'

'Then perhaps I should go round to the side entrance,' Maria murmured. 'After all, I don't want to cause any trouble.'

'Nonsense! Anyway, you're not just going to be any old servant. You've come to see Mama about the lady's maid position, right?'

Maria smiled, liking this unconventional young man more and more.

'Yes, my half-brother, Will Croft, arranged it.'

Did Maria imagine it, or did Daniel Pennington's expression change, the dark eyes narrowing, the finely shaped lips tightening a little.

'Oh, yes, Croft the farmer.'

Then his face lightened again.

'But I'm being a rotten host, Miss Croft. Come on, let me take you in and bring you to Mama's room.'

Maria allowed him to link her

arm through his and lead her into Pennington Hall.

'My name isn't Croft, by the way. It's Oates, Maria Oates. Will and I have the same mother, but different fathers.'

'That probably explains why you look nothing like him.'

He was moving quickly as he spoke, and Maria had to increase her pace to match his.

'I think Mama will still be in her dressing-room.' He grinned ruefully. 'She's not the earliest of risers, but then, sometimes I think that she finds her days rather long. After all, there's not really a great deal to interest a lady of the so-called Quality.'

Maria was now following him up a highly-polished, sweeping oak staircase, with elaborately-carved banisters.

'Your family seems to like its carvings,' she remarked, thinking of the two ferocious-looking lions on the pillars outside.

'Oh, Father did some travelling in

Africa and India in his younger days. I think he formed a liking for them then. Right then, here we are, Miss Maria Oates. This is Mother's room.'

He tapped on the door where they'd stopped and Maria felt butterflies fluttering haplessly in her stomach.

'Who is it?' a somewhat languid voice queried from inside the room.

'Miss Maria Oates is here to see you, Mama. I understand that she has an interview for a position as lady's maid.'

'Oh, yes,' the voice called back. 'I quite forgot the girl was coming. Give me five minutes, Daniel.'

Daniel Pennington raised an eyebrow and shook his head, his lips quirking at the corners, but he spoke obediently enough.

'Certainly, Mama.'

Then he turned to Maria.

'Well, it looks like you're stuck with me for the next five minutes, or, more likely ten. Mother's never been much of a time keeper. So what would you like to do? A cup of tea or coffee, perhaps? Or maybe you'd rather have a short, conducted tour of the house.'

'The latter, please,' Maria replied.

'Right then, we'll go back downstairs, and you can have a quick look around. There won't be time to go over the whole place.'

He pulled a face.

'Do you know, the house area is close on quarter of a mile, all told. It's ridiculously big for a family of our size, but you know how it is. Papa inherited the old place from his papa, and so on.'

Maria stifled a laugh, and Daniel looked at her sharply.

'Did I say something amusing?'

'Not really. I was just thinking how far apart our worlds are. My father didn't even own the little, terraced house which I grew up in.'

'Were you very poor?' he asked, as he took her arm and led her back down the staircase. 'May I call you Maria, by the way?'

'Certainly,' Maria replied, then, with a flash of humour, 'After all, you are my prospective employer's son, so I suppose that gives you the right to call me what you will!'

'Not in my opinion,' he replied, quickly. 'I should hate to think that I give the impression that someone looking for a job here is so much my social inferior that I can trample all over her.'

'You didn't, and I wouldn't let you do so anyway,' Maria replied, with a smile.

Then, thinking that she might perhaps have appeared too forward, she quickly changed the subject by answering his earlier questions.

'By your standards, I would imagine that you would call us workhouse poor. And yet, where we lived was considered quite respectable by most people. My father was in regular employment, and we were always able to pay our rent, and have enough food on the table.'

'Then I suppose you were quite lucky

after all,' he replied, musingly. 'You know, I hate the thought of people being so poor that they have to go to the workhouse.'

He swept a hand around encompassing the impressive hallway of Pennington Hall.

'It seems so unfair that we have all this, while other people are hungry.'

Unconsciously, he had raised his voice, and before Maria had a chance to answer, she became aware of a tinkling laugh, and an exquisitely gowned creature of about seventeen came towards them.

'Heaven's above, Daniel, are you holding forth with all your rubbish again!' the apparition said. 'Why, your poor guest must be bored quite silly!'

Then her eyes narrowed.

'Who is she, anyway? And what, pray, are you doing coming downstairs with her? Surely you haven't been sufficiently remiss as to smuggle a young lady up to your room right under Mama's nose!'

'Felicity, you will learn to guard your tongue and mind your manners!' Daniel snapped. 'Maria, I must apologise for my young sister. She tends to be somewhat outspoken, and to speak before thinking.'

'Huh! And aren't you the one to talk about that!' Felicity Pennington exclaimed indignantly. 'Why, you have poor Papa almost driven to distraction with your hare-brained, radical ideas! But enough of all that. Aren't you going to formally introduce me to your friend? I must say that I cannot recall ever having seen her anywhere before, and, as you know, I have a remarkable memory for faces.'

'Yes, of course,' Daniel replied. 'Felicity, this is Miss Maria Oates. Maria, my younger sister, Felicity Pennington.'

'I'm very pleased to meet you,' Felicity said, extending her hand.

Maria took it.

'And I you, Miss Pennington,' she said.

'You're not from the island, are you?' the younger girl said. 'If I'm not very much mistaken, that's a Scottish accent.'

'Yes, Miss Pennington. I came to the island from Ardrossan, yesterday.'

Felicity put a hand to her mouth.

'Then you must be the person Mama's interviewing for a position here.'

She rounded on Daniel, her small dark eyes furious.

'Good grief, Daniel, have you taken leave of your senses? Escorting a servant around the house just as if she were gentry, and introducing her to your sister as though she's my social equal! Well, the only thing I can say is it's a good job that Papa is out today supervising things at the mine, otherwise he'd have had a good deal to say about this little charade.'

She picked up her gown and walked away quickly, her head held at a haughty angle.

'No doubt you'll see fit to tell him,

with a few choice embellishments!' Daniel called after her, his voice deep with anger.

'Daniel Pennington, if you weren't my only brother, I vow that I'd positively hate you!'

And she flounced off, with a rustle of petticoats, leaving Maria suffering agonies of embarrassment.

'Oh, dear, I wasn't thinking. I shouldn't have agreed to your suggestion to show me the house, I should have remembered my position.'

'You should have done exactly as you did!' he replied, grimly. 'You have nothing to upbraid yourself about, Maria. That little exchange was entirely Felicity's fault. She's a mean-spirited creature, I have to admit, even if she is my own sister. She's been horribly spoiled. Take no notice of her. She'll grow up sometime. Now, I'll just give you a quick look around downstairs.'

As he spoke, he flung open a heavy, panelled oak door.

'This is the ceremonial dining-room,

or, at least, that's what I call it, since it's the one that's used for formal dinners.'

'It's a very beautiful room,' Maria said.

Her voice was slightly awestruck, as she took in the long, highly-polished, mahogany table, laid out for dinner with expensive silver cutlery and crystal glasses, the silk wallpaper on which hung a painting which she recognised as being by Constable.

'It's too cold for my taste,' Daniel said dismissing it contemptuously, as he closed the door. 'But then, apart from my own quarters which I've decorated to suit myself, the whole house is cold and impersonal.'

They went on to look at the small dining-room, which was used for more informal family meals, the drawing-room, Mrs Pennington's sitting-room, the library and the billiard room. By this time, Maria was beginning to feel totally overawed. It was definitely more grand than she had expected.

'Do you think I should be going to see your mother yet?' she asked, not sure how much time had elapsed, but feeling that at least ten minutes must have done so.

Daniel sighed.

'Yes, I suppose so.'

He looked down at her from his height of just over six feet, his expression meaningful.

'After all, I don't want to upset dear Mama, otherwise she might not engage you, and that would surely be my loss . . . '

4

Mrs Pennington had the rather impatient air of someone who has been kept waiting, and isn't used to it. She was a tall, stately-looking woman with dark hair pulled back from her slightly angular face and arranged in a neat bun.

'So, at last!' she cried, imperiously, rising from the chaise-longue.

'I'm sorry if I've kept you waiting, ma'am,' Maria replied.

Things didn't seem to be getting off to a very good start! True, Daniel was handsome and charming, but she'd unwittingly made an enemy of Felicity, and it looked as if Mrs Pennington was none too pleased with her either. But to Maria's surprise, the older woman smiled.

'Oh, don't worry, I'm not blaming you. I know my own son's faults, and he has plenty, more's the pity.'

She eyed Maria keenly.

'You've a smart appearance, haven't you? You're not a conventional beauty, yet you have something. Actually, if one didn't know better, I would say it was breeding. You hold yourself well, and have delicate bone structure, despite your height.'

Maria felt stirrings of anger. Was this woman deliberately goading her? Her thoughts must have shown on her face, because Mrs Pennington actually gave a slight chuckle.

'I suppose my comments might have sounded condescending, but I actually meant them as a compliment. After all, I don't want some hulking, raw-boned creature pulling a hairbrush through my hair!'

As she spoke, Mrs Pennington sat down again, and with a quick flick of her slender wrist, indicated a hard-backed chair for Maria to sit on.

'Now, to get to the business in hand. We were informed by your brother,

Farmer Croft, that you have worked in Scotland as a lady's maid, and are anxious to find a similar position here. Do you have a reference from your previous position?'

Maria bit her lip. Here it was, the moment she had been waiting for, dreading. It was no use. No-one was going to employ her when they found out that she had no reference from the Macphersons, even though she'd been there three years.

She had one from her previous position, as a maidservant in the home of a Mrs Agnes Stewart, and one from the school which she had attended up until the age of fourteen, but Mrs Pennington was sure to wonder what she had done to upset the Macphersons. Mrs Pennington pursed her lips, and tapped her knee impatiently.

'Well, girl, I'm waiting! Do you have a reference from your last employer or not? You're blushing, which is always a tell-tale sign. Is it so bad that you're ashamed to show it to me?'

Maria took a deep breath.

'I don't have a reference from my previous employer, although I was there for three years. I do, however, have one from a Mrs Agnes Stewart, for whom I worked when I left school, and a reference from the headmaster of my school, if you would care to look at them, ma'am?'

Mrs Pennington inclined her head.

'Yes, bring them over to me, girl.'

Maria opened her reticule and took out the two envelopes, then she walked over to Mrs Pennington and handed them to her, turning away as the older woman read them.

'Exemplary,' Mrs Pennington announced, handing them back to Maria. 'So, what went wrong at your last position?'

'I had a . . . a disagreement with the lady I was working for.'

'That tells me nothing!' Mrs Pennington snapped. 'If you want this position, then you'll tell me the truth, and in plain language. You're an intelligent girl, and should understand that I have to know about the backgrounds of the people I employ.'

'I'm sorry, ma'am. It's just that it's rather embarrassing,' Maria began, haltingly.

Mrs Pennington leaned forward.

'Ah, ha! You weren't sent packing because you had a crush on your mistress' son, by any chance? I won't have you making sheep's eyes at Daniel!'

The remark was a little too near the truth. Maria had found Daniel Pennington attractive, but she certainly hadn't made sheep's eyes at him! Oh no, she knew her place in life better than to think of doing that, and besides, there was Rob Cregeen to think of.

'I certainly was not dismissed for such a thing! In fact, my dismissal was quite unfair, and concerned Mrs Macpherson's husband, who was a known womaniser.'

Mrs Pennington laughed.

'All right, you sound so indignant

that I believe you, and you certainly won't find Mr Pennington senior susceptible to your charms. My husband gathered from Farmer Croft that you wish to commence work as soon as possible. I take it that is correct?'

'Yes, ma'am.'

'Very, well then, I'm prepared to give you six months' trial. You can go back to the farm and get your things and move in today. My previous lady's maid left without giving notice, and it's most inconvenient having to make do with one of the housemaids. You will receive a half-day off each week, and alternate Sundays, although you will be expected to accompany me to church each Sunday, whether it's your day off or not.

'You will receive a wage of five shillings a week, all found. By all found, I mean that you will receive your keep, and will be given two uniforms, and changes of linen. Right then. You may go now. I'll expect you back here early this afternoon.'

'Yes, ma'am, thank you,' Maria replied.

She went back to Laxey station, where she took a tram back to Maughold, and walked the comparatively short distance to the farm. Jessie saw her coming from the window, and ran out to greet her.

'Well, how did it go?'

'I've got the job, and five shillings a week all found. I'm to move in today.'

Jessie hugged her.

'Oh Maria, I'm so happy for you. That's a really good opportunity.'

She led her daughter into the farmhouse.

'Come and tell Isobel. I know she's going to be just as pleased as I am.'

'That's wonderful news, Maria!' Isobel exclaimed. 'And she's being quite generous to you, as well. You certainly must have made a good impression on her.'

'I don't know about that, but I certainly didn't make a very good impression on Felicity Pennington.'

And she went on to tell them of her encounter with the youngest Pennington.

'She's a trouble-maker, that one,' Isobel said. 'I'd keep well out of her way, if I was you. A pity her father doesn't find a husband for the young minx.'

'Maria will be serving Mrs Pennington, so she shouldn't need to have too much contact with the daughter,' Jessie said. 'And one half-day off every week, plus alternate Sundays! That really is generous of her. Well, at least we'll not be losing sight of you when you go to live at the manor.'

'No, of course you won't, Mother!'

Then a thought struck her.

'Rob Cregeen is going to call here to see me on Thursday. Will you explain to him why I can't be here? I don't want him to think that I've just let him down.'

'You know I will. Anyway, who knows? You may just be lucky and have Thursday as your half-day off.'

‘I hardly think so, seeing as I’m only starting on Wednesday.’

As it happened, Mrs Pennington asked Maria which afternoon she would like for her half-day as soon as she arrived back at Pennington Hall that afternoon.

Maria hesitated. Was it being too presumptuous to ask for Thursday when she’d only just started? Oh, well, perhaps if she explained why, Mrs Pennington wouldn’t think too badly of her, even if she didn’t actually give her permission.

Mrs Pennington looked at her consideringly.

‘I admire your spirit, girl, and who am I to keep two young folk apart? Yes, go and meet your young man tomorrow, and at the same time you can see your mother, and put her mind at rest by telling her that you’re settling in well.’

Maria was in good spirits as she left Pennington Hall shortly after one o’clock the following day, and took the tram back to Maughold.

She had already been formally introduced to Mr Pennington, and Felicity, who looked through her, and said, catchingly, 'I don't mingle with servants.'

That remark, however, had been the young lady's downfall. Mrs Pennington had been most annoyed, and had told her daughter that greeting a servant courteously on introduction was not classed as mingling and that she had been very rude towards Maria.

Mr Pennington had been polite, but had looked at her as if she was very much his social inferior, which, of course, she was. As for Daniel, well, fortunately, she hadn't found herself alone with him again, although she'd fancied once or twice that his dark eyes had lingered on her rather longer than they should.

But she shouldn't be thinking of Daniel, or the Penningtons on her day off. She should be thinking of Rob, and how she hadn't had to let him down after all.

Jessie and Isobel were surprised when Maria walked in.

'My word, I was right after all and you did get Thursday afternoon off,' her mother said when she greeted her.

'If you don't mind, I'll just go upstairs and freshen up before Rob arrives.'

'Here then, take this kettle with you. You'll find a bowl in the room you used when you first arrived.'

'Thanks, Isobel.'

With a smile for her mother and sister-in-law, Maria took the kettle and went upstairs. Isobel and Jessie exchanged meaningful glances.

'It looks as if young Rob has made quite an impression on Maria,' Isobel observed wryly.

'Yes, he does, doesn't he?'

'There's no love lost between Rob and Will, you know,' Isobel said. 'Not that I blame Rob.'

She went on to tell Jessie how Rob's young brother, Johnnie, had been caught in the man trap, and that although Will had been acquitted of any negligence, there had been talk.

'In fact, I think it's pretty brave of Rob to actually come here. He must think quite a lot of your Maria to do so.'

'Well, he didn't strike me as a coward,' Jessie admitted. 'Anyway, time will tell, after all, they only just met on the crossing. They'll need more time to get to know one another.'

'Yes, of course,' Isobel agreed. 'And the Penningtons keep a number of servants. Who knows who Maria may meet up at the hall?'

Rob arrived before Maria had completed her toilette, and Isobel went upstairs to tell her that he was there.

'But don't worry,' she added, smiling good-naturedly at Maria's look of consternation. 'He's quite comfortable, sitting in the parlour drinking tea and eating a scone with strawberry jam and clotted cream. Your mother's with him, and they seem to be chatting together just as if they've known each other for years.'

Rob stood up as they entered the parlour, his likeable features breaking into a wide smile, while his deep blue eyes shone with admiration as they lingered on Maria.

'You're looking lovely, Miss Maria. It'll be an honour for me to escort two such attractive females.'

He smiled at Jessie, but she was shaking her head.

'No, young man, there's no need for you to feel that you have to take me along with you. Isobel and I have spent precious little time together over the years, and have a lot of catching up to do.'

Rob couldn't quite prevent a look of pleasure from spreading over his open features, but he did have the good manners to say, 'Are you quite sure, Mrs Oates? I'd planned that we would take the electric tram into Ramsey, and then take afternoon tea there.'

'Perhaps another time,' Jessie answered,

with a smile. 'It sounds very pleasant, but I'm sure that you two young people will enjoy yourself much more if you haven't got an old woman tagging along. Now, be off with you. It's quite a pleasant afternoon. You should make the most of it.'

Maria really enjoyed her afternoon with Rob, who proved to be very good company. He regaled her with incidents from his working life on the steam packet vessels.

She was also impressed with Ramsey, the largest town on the northern part of the island. They strolled along the promenade, and went for a walk along the pier. Then Rob suggested that they take tea. They sat in the front room of a small, eighteenth-century, thatched-roof cottage café and ate the most delicious home-made scones.

'What time do you have to be back at the hall?' Rob asked.

'I have until eight o'clock tomorrow morning, actually. Mrs Pennington said that she won't need me until then. I can either go back to the Hall and sleep there this evening, or stay at the farm, just as long as I'm punctual in the morning. That is, if Will agrees to me staying overnight.'

The mischief was gone from Rob's face, as he said, angrily, 'What do you mean? Didn't he make you welcome? If he was rude to you, or even lifts a finger towards you, I swear I'll . . . '

'He doesn't want me living at the farm,' Maria interrupted, 'but I think that's mainly because he doesn't want an extra mouth to feed. Seeing as I've got a job so quickly, and won't be dependent on him, he probably won't mind me staying the occasional night there.

'Mind you, I think I should go back to the Hall this evening. After all, it was very kind of Mrs Pennington to agree to let me take this afternoon off. I don't want her to think that I'm imposing on her generosity.'

Rob inclined his head as he replied. 'That's fair enough. She must be a bit more lenient than her husband. I don't know him personally, of course, but I know several of the lads who work in his mines. They reckon he's a hard taskmaster.'

'I've only met him once,' Maria replied.

'And what about young Mr Daniel? Have you met him yet?'

To her embarrassment, Maria found herself stammering slightly as she replied.

'Oh, yes, I met him when I first arrived, and he seemed quite different to the others, much more human.'

'Aye, they say he's a fine man. He's not too keen to go into the mines, I gather, though there's many who would like him to.'

'Does his father want him to?'

Rob spread his hands helplessly.

'You're the one who's working there, Maria. You should know more than the likes of me!'

'Well, I haven't been there very long yet, have I? And besides, the position

I hold is rather a strange one. I'm not good enough to take my meals with the family, but, as yet, I haven't eaten with the other servants, either. A tray is sent to my room.'

'That must be a bit lonely for you.'

Maria shook her head.

'Not so far. But I suppose it would be nice to get to know some of the others, seeing as I know so few people on the island.'

'Are you off duty this Sunday?'

'No, it will be the following one.'

'Well, that's better for me. The boats will be starting to go quiet by then, and I'll be off every Sunday. What do you say to coming to dinner at my parents'? I know that they'd be delighted to have you, and then you can start getting to know some people.

'I'm the eldest of my family, and I have three younger brothers, and three sisters, ranging from three to twenty-one. Mind you, the two elder girls are married, and my brother, Joe, so that only leaves the four of us still at home with the parents. But meeting them would give you a start.'

'It must be nice to be part of a big family,' Maria replied, rather wistfully. 'I always felt as if I was an only one. Of course, there was Will, but he left home when I was only ten, and I've never felt that I had anything in common with him anyway.'

Rob's expression darkened.

'You certainly haven't, thank goodness!'

He reached across the table, and, taking hold of Maria's hand, squeezed it gently.

'I'm very glad that you decided to come to the Isle of Man, Maria Oates.'

Maria found the next few weeks at Pennington Hall rather trying. Mrs Pennington, she discovered, was inclined to be somewhat moody. One day, she would be all over Maria, and the next would find fault with almost everything she did.

Maria also came to the conclusion

that the Penningtons' marriage was not a very happy one, and that this contributed to Rachel Pennington's moods.

Felicity still spent her days in the idle pursuit of pleasure, and was starting to make demands on her mother's maid. Maria felt sure that she only did this because she was so bored that baiting Maria had become a new hobby for her.

Felicity frequently went to visit the neighbouring gentry, and would make a point of taking Maria with her, then took pleasure in belittling her at every opportunity. Felicity was also fond of riding, and decreed that Maria must learn to ride, as it would be a novelty for her to be accompanied by a lady's maid rather than a groom.

Maria had always been rather frightened of horses, which pleased Felicity even more, particularly as Maria took two or three tumbles. One morning, she landed in some water-logged muddy earth, after a few days of heavy rain. It was on this occasion that Daniel Pennington had decided to join them, which made Maria feel even more humiliated.

He didn't laugh, as Felicity invariably did. Instead, he gave his younger sister a black look, dismounted and, squatting down, reached out a hand and pulled Maria to her feet.

'You're all right, I trust?' His face, and voice, were both anxious. 'You didn't seem to fall too heavily, but if you're in pain, I can ride over and fetch Dr Roger.'

Maria shook her head.

'No, there's no need for that.'

She looked down at herself ruefully. The rather old-fashioned riding habit, which Felicity had purchased second-hand for her, was caked with clinging, slimy mud.

'I look a positive sight. I think, if you don't mind, Miss Felicity, I'll go and change. As you have your brother with you, perhaps you won't require me to join you on your ride today.'

'You'll do nothing of the sort!' Felicity snapped, petulantly. 'It's hardly my fault if you're such a rotten horsewoman that you can't stay in the saddle. Now, remount at once! You're wasting our time.'

Maria's lips tightened, but she inclined her head, and was about to move towards the mare when Daniel thrust his hand under her arm and stopped her.

'Stop being such a spoiled, little brat, Felicity!' he exclaimed. 'Surely even you can see that Maria can hardly ride on like this. She must be feeling most uncomfortable, never mind shaken, and, quite probably, bruised. If you want to continue with your ride, go and get one of the grooms to accompany you. Speaking for myself, I'm going to see Maria safely inside. What she needs now is a hot bath, and a rest. I will inform Mama.'

And with that, he gently propelled Maria back towards the house. Felicity's voice followed them.

'What's the matter, Daniel? Are you smitten with the servant girl? Because I can tell you now, neither Mama or Papa is going to be very pleased!'

5

Maria thought about that remark of Felicity's many times over the next few months. She was very aware that Daniel singled her out whenever he could, and she could tell by the warmth of his gaze when he looked at her, that he was attracted to her.

She realised, too, that she found him attractive. But such thoughts were dangerous. He was the son of a wealthy mine owner, and she was a servant. There couldn't possibly be any future for them together.

She was now spending all her free time with Rob, and for the past few weeks, he had been hinting at marriage, or at least, to become engaged. Maria was fond of him, and she liked the Cregeen family, whom she had now met several times. Yet she hesitated.

It wasn't that she wanted to spend

the rest of her life working for the Penningtons, she didn't. But it seemed so final, somehow, to commit herself to Rob when she wasn't totally sure that she loved him. It had all happened so quickly. And yet, on the very rare occasion when she allowed herself to think about Daniel, and imagine he was an equal, she knew that it would be very easy to fall in love with him.

Fortunately, Daniel wasn't at the Hall so much these days. His father had insisted that he go to a colliery in Wales to learn more about mining. Pennington Hall seemed very empty without his presence.

Maria was in her small bedroom one evening, doing some intricate needlework for Mrs Pennington, when there was a tap on the door.

'I won't be a moment,' she called, wondering who it could be at this time of night.

Putting the gown she was working on carefully on the bed, she went to the door and opened it, to find Jenny, one of the maids from downstairs, standing outside.

'Why Jenny, what is it?' Maria asked, noticing the girl's distress.

'It's your young man, Maria. He arrived here in quite a state, demanding to see you. Well, there was a bit of a to-do.'

She lowered her voice, with a slightly apprehensive glance behind her.

'Come in, Jenny, and close the door. Then you can tell me just what all this is about.'

Maria felt her heart beginning to race. What on earth had happened? Had Rob taken leave of his senses to turn up here, uninvited, at a time when he knew she would be working.

'Mr Pennington was annoyed that Rob called at the main entrance. You see, he happened to be in the hall at the time, and answered the door himself. Rob wasn't having any of it. He said he was staying until he saw you. Well, their raised voices brought Mrs Pennington out from the drawing-room, and she wanted to know what was going on. Rob told her that there'd been an accident at sea.'

Jenny's voice faltered, and she dropped her eyes.

'Apparently, someone had just come to the Cregeen's cottage and told them the body of Ben Cregeen, Rob's father, had been washed up on Cornaa beach.'

Maria sank down on to the bed, unmindful of Rachel Pennington's gown. Her face had drained of colour, as she pictured bluff, hearty Ben Cregeen, who had always teased her when she had gone with Rob to the Cregeen's cottage for dinner.

'Rob will be devastated,' she said, at last. 'I must go to see him. Where is he, Jenny?'

'Mr Pennington was all for sending him down to the servants' quarters, once he finally agreed that he could see you at all. But Mrs Pennington said that he could go into the Blue Room, and that I was to fetch you, and tell you to go down there straightaway.'

'Thank you, Jenny. I'll go immediately.'

When Maria entered the room, Rob was standing in front of the huge fireplace, twisting his cap in his hands, and looking decidedly ill-at-ease and miserable.

Maria ran over to him.

'Oh, Rob, I'm so very, very sorry. Come and sit down.'

'Pa had been at sea for several days,' Rob was saying, 'but that wasn't really so unusual. The men often go to the coasts of Scotland or Ireland to fish.'

He stroked his chin, where faint blond stubble showed, thoughtfully.

'Mind you, I suppose it was a bit unusual for this time of year, seeing as it's coming up to Christmas. The Irish Sea is not known for benevolence in winter.'

Then he covered his face with his hands, his shoulders shaking. Maria went over to him, and put her arm round his shoulders. Rob turned her hand palm upwards and kissed it.

'You must agree to marry me now,

Maria. I couldn't stand it if I lost you as well. I was very close to the old man, you know that, and poor Ma, well, she's fair breaking her heart.'

'I'll go and see her on my half-day off, this Friday,' Maria said quickly.

She knew that Mrs Cregeen would be devastated. They'd seemed to her to be a couple who were devoted to one another.

'Yes, do that, love, she'd be very glad, I know she would. But what about you and me? I know I haven't had such a good education as you, Maria, but I do truly love you, and will look after you for the rest of my days. Surely that must count for something.'

Maria felt her heart going out to him.

'Oh, Rob, I'm not sure that I'm quite ready for marriage just yet, but I'll tell you what. If you like, we can get engaged.'

Rob stood up, and drew her into his arms, his lips coming down firmly on hers. Then he put her gently away from him.

'Aye, lass, that'll do very well, at least for now!'

Daniel returned from Wales the following day. He hadn't been expected until the start of the next week, but on his father's testy question as to why he was home sooner, Daniel replied nonchalantly.

'I'm a quick learner, Papa. Mr Griffiths decided that there was little more he could teach me.'

'And have you made your mind up now? Are you going to take over the running of Snaefell and Laxey mines?'

'I'll certainly look into the possibility,' Daniel replied. 'And now, Papa, if you don't object, I would like to take a bath and change. I've been travelling for several, long hours.'

As he left the room, Daniel winked at Maria, who immediately dropped her eyes. Oh, but he was incorrigible! So why was it that her heart had started to beat a little faster when he had entered the room?

Then came a sobering thought. Although she was as yet not wearing a ring, and hadn't told anyone about it, she was engaged to Rob Cregeen. She had given him her word, and it was not in her nature to break it.

Mrs Pennington had been kind and thoughtful towards Maria that morning, when Maria brought her mistress breakfast in bed. This was the custom, shortly after ten o'clock, unless Mrs Pennington had any earlier engagements.

'Your young man's family must be very upset at the loss of the head of the house,' Mrs Pennington said, as she sat up in bed.

'Yes, I would imagine so, ma'am. I intend to go and see Mrs Cregeen on Friday afternoon.'

Mrs Pennington shook her head.

'No, don't wait until Friday. Go this afternoon. That may help to cheer her up. And you can also tell her from me that I will give you the day off to attend the funeral. No, better still, you can accompany me. As the largest landowners in the area, it's only fitting that there should be a representative from the Pennington family there.'

'Thank you, ma'am. That's very kind of you.'

'Oh, not at all. Tell me, do you intend to marry this young fellow, what's his name, Robert?'

'Yes, Robert, ma'am, although he's known as Rob.'

Maria hesitated momentarily, then decided that she had better tell Mrs Pennington that she and Rob had decided to get engaged, although, of course, she had no ring as yet.

'That's wonderful news, and I wish you every happiness. Mind you, I trust that you don't intend to marry and start a family rightaway. You're proving an admirable lady's maid, and I shall be very loath to lose you.'

'No, I have no intention of marrying in the foreseeable future.'

When she arrived at the Cregeens'

that afternoon, she found Lily Cregeen with eyes streaked red from crying.

'It was such a shock, such a shock,' she murmured, over and over again. 'And he wasn't an old man, my Bob. He was only just turned forty three. I don't know, sometimes you wonder how God can be so cruel.'

'At least you've got the children for company,' Maria murmured, picking up three-year-old Amy, who was looking as if she, too, might burst into tears at any moment.

'Yes, I know, and though I love them all dearly, I can't help but wonder how we're all going to manage with poor Bob gone. Rob is very good, and makes a fair bit of money in the summer, but in winter, the hours are cut so he doesn't bring home that much. The only other one out working is Billy, and he doesn't make that much as a farmhand on old Tom Crosby's farm.'

'Perhaps I could help you out a bit.'

But Lily shook her head, and patted Maria's hand.

'No, love, we'll manage somehow. If I say so myself, I'm a very good cook, and now with the trams coming through Laxey, there's plenty of visitors. I might open up my front room as a little café.'

She seemed to brighten up a little, as she continued.

'After all, you want to save all you can for your wedding. Rob was telling me that the two of you are getting engaged, and right pleased to hear it, I was, too! You'll make him a fine wife.'

Maria smiled a little uncertainly. She only hoped that Mrs Cregeen, and, more important, Rob, wouldn't be disappointed in her. Mrs Cregeen insisted that Maria take tea with her, and they were sitting drinking tea and eating sandwiches when Rob came in. He smiled at his mother and Maria.

'I've been into Douglas to get the ring,' he said with such excitement.

As he spoke, he reached into his trouser pocket and drew out a little box, which he handed to Maria.

'I hope you like it and it fits you all right. I had to guess the size, but Mr Issacs, the jeweller, said that it can be altered easily enough should it be too big.'

Maria was torn between feelings of excitement and unworthiness as she opened the ring box. It was a fairly simple gold and diamond ring, but to her, it was beautiful. Tentatively, she slipped it on to the third finger of her left hand. It was a little too big, and she had to take it off again, in case it fell off and she lost it.

Rob looked a bit disappointed, so she quickly pointed out that it was much better that it was too large than too small, otherwise it would have been more difficult to do anything about it.

'That's true,' he agreed. 'But you do like it, don't you? You're not annoyed that I just went off and got it without you?'

'I think it's beautiful,' Maria replied, truthfully, and Rob came over and kissed her cheek, oblivious of his mother, and two younger sisters watching.

'I'll take it back there tonight. They're open until nine o'clock.'

'Oh, it's all right. I don't want you to have to go back into Douglas specially. Wait until you're going anyway.'

But Rob shook his head stubbornly.

'No, I'd rather that it was altered rightaway. That way you'll be wearing my ring, and I'll know that you're really mine.'

'Well, I suppose I should be going. I want to call in at the farm and see my mother before I go back to Pennington Hall.'

'Now that we're engaged, I think that I should call in at the farm, too. As you know, there's no love lost between me and Will Croft, but he is your half-brother. I suppose that when we're married, that will make him a kind of relative. It's time we made peace.'

'I'd really rather prepare the way

first,' Maria admitted. 'After all, none of them knows anything about our engagement yet.'

Rob hesitated, and Maria saw her opportunity, and pressed home the point.

'Look, I'm off this Sunday. Why don't you come to tea with us then? I'll tell them when I call there tonight.'

'Yes, I suppose you're right. All right then. I'll see you on Sunday.'

When she reached the farmhouse, Jessie was polishing the brass ornaments in the parlour, and turned, duster in hand, as her daughter came into the room.

'Why, Maria, love, what a nice surprise. I didn't know you were off work today. I thought you were coming here tomorrow.'

Maria quickly told her about Bob Cregeen's tragic death, and that Mrs Pennington had given her a half day today instead of tomorrow so that she could call on the grieving widow. Jessie looked slightly perplexed.

'Well, that was very kind of her, but I can't really see what it's got to do with you, Maria. Oh, I know you and Rob are friends, but they must have people that they've known for a lot longer. Why did Mrs Pennington say that you could go there rightaway?'

Maria sensed her mother's agitation. Somehow, she'd known that Jessie wasn't too pleased at her association with Rob, even though he was a good, upright young man. She took a deep breath.

'She told me to go and see Mrs Cregeen because Rob and I have got engaged.'

Jessie stood as if turned to stone, then she shook her head.

'It won't work out, you know! Oh, I've nothing against the lad, but I just don't feel that he's right for you.'

She eyed her daughter keenly.

'Did you do this out of pity, Maria? Did you agree to a betrothal when he told you that his father had drowned?'

'No, no! Of course not,' Maria

protested, but even to her own ears, her voice sounded uncertain.

Jessie looked at her sadly.

'I've said to Rob that he can come here on Sunday and have tea with us. Do you think that'll be all right?'

'I'll speak to your brother about it. Oh, Maria, I'm sorry for being such a kill-joy, love. If you want to marry Rob Cregeen, then I'll give you my blessing. I suppose the trouble is that I've always been over ambitious for you, but you're right. He's a good lad, steady, and a hard worker. You could do a lot worse.'

'You've made me feel a lot better about everything now. But what about Will? Do you think that he'll be prepared to bury the hatchet and accept Rob?'

'Will is my son, and will do as I say,' Jessie replied.

6

Tea at the Croft's farm went off much better than Maria had thought, with both Rob and Will making a determined effort to be pleasant to one another, although there was the occasional frown from Rob when he didn't think anyone else was watching.

Of course, that was only to be expected. Maria had grown quite fond of young Johnnie, and was horrified by the lad's leg injury. He could only get along with the aid of crutches, and would never be able to go out to work. However, he had a good pair of hands and a talent for carving wooden figures, which were sold in the local shops.

It was when Maria and Rob were on the tram, Maria on her way back to Pennington Hall, and Rob to his home, that Rob dropped his bombshell.

'I've got something to tell you,

Maria,' he said hesitantly, twisting his cap in his hands as he spoke. 'I'm not sure how you're going to take it.'

Maria looked at him anxiously.

'Then tell me as quickly as possible.'

'I'm going to work for the Penningtons, in the mines.'

Maria was temporarily speechless, and when she did find her voice, it came out as little more than a husky murmur.

'But why, Rob? I thought you liked being at sea.'

'The work's uncertain in the winter, love. It was all right while Pa was alive, but now with him gone and me soon to be a married man, I need a more regular source of income. The pay isn't as good as what I earn in the summer, but it's year-round work, and that counts for a lot these days.'

Maria looked at him sadly.

'I've handed my notice in at the shipping company and to be quite honest with you, I reckon they were glad enough to take it. They don't do a lot in winter, as I've said, and there's always plenty of lads prepared to take seasonal work when it's busier.'

As the tram jolted to a halt, Maria's face suddenly drained of colour. She was remembering Nellie Wheeler's words — that someone whom she cared for would die, and that there would be smoke, fumes and water around. Could Nellie have had a premonition about Rob, and the mines?

Rob took her arm and helped her off the tram.

'What on earth's the matter?' he asked, noticing her pallor. 'You look as if you've seen a ghost.'

Quickly, Maria told him how her friend's mother had told her fortune before she left Ardrossan, and what she'd said. To her consternation, Rob threw back his head and laughed heartily.

'What an absolute load of rubbish! Surely an educated girl like you doesn't believe that nonsense.'

Maria blushed.

'I suppose it does sound a bit fanciful,' she admitted, feeling a bit stupid. 'Nevertheless, Rob, you must admit that mining is a dangerous occupation.'

'My love, what job is totally safe? Certainly not one at sea!'

Suddenly, she understood. His father's death by drowning was the real reason why he now wanted a land job. And who was she to try and dissuade him? Rob had been deeply affected by his father's death. Perhaps he would forget quicker if he didn't have the sea to remind him.

She waved him goodbye as the tram moved away, and turned in the direction of Pennington Hall.

Maria's mind was in a turmoil as she walked up the drive. She was still sure that Rob was making a mistake in going to work in the Pennington mines, but she was now equally sure that nothing she could say would make him change his mind.

She looked down at Rob's ring, which

now fitted her finger perfectly, and sighed. What would the future hold for them? Then she jumped, clasping her hand to her heart, as a figure appeared beside her suddenly.

'Oh, but you gave me quite a turn, Mr Daniel!' she exclaimed.

Daniel Pennington's handsome face mirrored irritation.

'For goodness' sake, Maria, call me Daniel. I don't hold with all this formal address nonsense!'

'Then you're the only person in your family who feels like that,' Maria couldn't help saying.

Daniel laughed.

'Yes, that's certainly true, but you can hardly hold my family against me, can you? After all, none of us can choose to whom we're born!'

Then his face tightened, as a shaft of moonlight caught Maria's left hand, as she occupied herself in fastening the loosened ribbon of her bonnet.

'What's that ring you're wearing?'

As he spoke, he turned her round to

face him. He caught hold of her hand and examined the ring more closely.

'Surely this is an engagement ring.'

Maria freed her hand from his grasp.

'Yes, it is,' she said, her voice not quite steady. 'I've just become engaged to Rob Cregeen.'

'Rob Cregeen? You mean the fellow whose father's funeral is tomorrow?'

Maria nodded wordlessly.

'But he was here this morning seeing my father about a job in the mines. I think father would have sent him packing, only I intervened.'

Maria lifted her face to meet Daniel's eyes.

'In that, I don't know whether you did him a favour or not. I can't think that he'll be happy working in the mines, although his father's death has affected him to such an extent that I don't think he could have remained working at sea, either.'

'I don't want to talk about him, Maria. I want to talk about you,' Daniel exclaimed. 'You're beautiful, and you're intelligent. Surely you don't want to throw yourself away by marrying a miner!'

Maria's dark eyes stared angrily at him.

'That remark was extremely patronising, sir, and you should apologise for it. Obviously, I wouldn't have become engaged to Rob Cregeen if I hadn't been very much in love with him.'

She turned on her heel, and hurried away from him, leaving him standing there looking after her, his expression curiously forlorn.

At first, Maria could feel nothing more than temper towards Daniel Pennington, which was perhaps just as well. It enabled her to hold herself totally aloof from him when he accompanied her and Mrs Pennington to Rob's father's funeral the following day.

But she found it impossible to remain distant when he was unfailingly kind to her, and protected her from the slights of his younger sister.

As Christmas drew near, the other Pennington daughter, Caroline, whom Maria hadn't yet met, came home, with her colonel husband. Soon, Maria knew that she was going to have yet more problems. Caroline was pleasant enough in a somewhat off-hand way, but it soon became clear that her husband, Simon Freestone, a handsome but weak fellow, was attracted to Maria and considered her fair game.

On Christmas Day, Maria was permitted to join in the family entertainments, and Simon quickly seized his opportunity, kissing her under the mistletoe. An embarrassed Maria struggled to free herself.

It was Daniel who came to her rescue, by pulling Freestone away by his starched collar. Simon, red-faced with anger, and too much port, rounded on his brother-in-law, out of the hearing of the others present.

'I say, old chap, that was a bit much, wasn't it? After all, it's Christmas day.

Surely it's a man's prerogative to kiss a pretty young girl under the mistletoe. And, when all's said and done, she's only a servant.'

Daniel's face darkened with temper.

'Maria is my mother's lady's maid, and a friend of mine. I'm warning you, Freestone, keep your hands off her!'

A knowing look spread across Simon Freestone's bland features.

'Ah, ha!' He chuckled. 'So that's the way the land lies, is it?'

He clapped his brother-in-law heartily across the shoulders.

'Well, let me know when you get tired of her, old man, will you?'

'If there was still such a custom as duelling, I swear I'd call you out for that remark!'

Daniel's voice was low and dangerous, and Simon Freestone blinked owlishly at him.

'Lord help it, man! You don't mean to tell me that you're genuinely enamoured of the girl?'

Daniel laughed mirthlessly.

'And if I am, it hardly makes any odds. Maria is engaged to be married.'

Simon glanced around to make sure that his wife was still deep in conversation with her mother, before continuing in hushed tones.

'What you need, my good man, is a night out on the town. Seeing it's Christmas, I doubt we'll be able to slip away until Wednesday, but then we could go into town and have some fun.'

He winked, and nudged Daniel meaningfully.

'Well, what do you say? Your sister's a fine woman and all that, but a man needs a change once in a while.'

Daniel Pennington looked at his brother-in-law in disgust, turning to where Maria was standing in fear and horror. He took hold of Maria's arm, leading her away. Then he paused, and said to the others over his shoulder, 'Maria and I are going into the gardens to take some fresh air. It's beginning to pall around here.'

Simon Freestone stared after him, open-mouthed.

'I'll have to fetch my coat,' Maria murmured. 'That is, if you think it'll be all right, my going out into the gardens without asking your mother's permission.'

Daniel threw a quick glance in his mother's direction, and was gratified to see that she was still deep in conversation with her elder daughter.

'Mama hasn't seen Caroline for a year before this visit. They've still got a lot of catching up to do. Don't worry, she won't notice, and dear little Felicity is too busy making sheep's eyes at Jimmy Costain to be aware of the fact that you've left the room.'

Maria smiled up at him.

'All right then. I'll just run upstairs and fetch my coat.

'Meet me at the side entrance. There'll be no chance of us being disturbed there.'

Daniel was waiting by the side door

when she got there, and he took hold of her hand.

'Come on,' he said, a touch of urgency in his voice. 'I don't want any of the servants to see us. Some of them are quite trustworthy, of course, but others would delight in running to Mama or Papa to tell them what their errant son is up to now!'

And just what was he up to, Maria began to wonder again as he ushered her through the door. She drew off her black, leather glove and looked down at the ring which graced her third finger — Rob's ring. Rob, who would start at the Pennington mines the day after Boxing Day, when the Christmas holidays were over.

Daniel caught her look, and smiled, although the smile didn't quite reach his eyes.

'Don't worry, Maria, I haven't forgotten that you're engaged to Robert Cregeen, and I assure you that I mean you no harm.'

He laughed somewhat mirthlessly.

'Mind you, I can't honestly say that I hold with such an engagement. He's a nice enough fellow, but he doesn't have your education and background, so I can't see that you're going to be very happy with him. But it's your choice, isn't it? And, after all, you do say that you love him.'

'You sound like my mother,' Maria admitted involuntarily, as Daniel took hold of her arm, and led her down a gravelled path flanked by trees. It was all a little bit ghostly.

'Your mother doesn't approve of your engagement?' he said, catching on to her words quickly.

'Oh, she's coming around to it,' Maria replied, with a slightly nervous laugh.

She didn't feel totally at ease with Daniel. Oh, he was unfailingly kind to her, but she knew that he found her attractive, and, what was more dangerous, she knew that she reciprocated his feelings, despite her engagement to Rob.

'Where are we going to, anyway?' she asked.

It was an icily cold night, and she could see her breath on the clear, frozen air.

'I'm taking you down to the summerhouse. It's too cold to walk around in the gardens for long, and it was becoming mightily oppressive stuck in there with the family.'

Maria had visited the summerhouse on a couple of occasions with Mrs Pennington when it had been a bright but cold day. Mrs Pennington had wanted to sit out there rather than in one of the stifling drawing-rooms indoors.

But now it was evening, and her companion was no longer Mrs Pennington.

'Sit down, Maria,' Daniel was saying, indicating one of the padded, cane chairs. 'I wanted us to be able to have a short time alone together because I have a Christmas present for you.'

'A Christmas present?' Maria echoed.

'Oh, but really, there's no need. I've already received a very nice pair of gloves from your mother.'

'Which is hardly the same thing,' he replied, taking a delicately wrapped package from his pocket. He leaned forward and put it into her hands. 'Happy Christmas, Maria, and many more of them!'

He leaned forward and placed the small package in her hands. Maria's fingers were trembling as she opened it.

'You shouldn't have done this,' she murmured. 'It isn't . . . well . . . fitting, and, besides, I have nothing for you.'

'Your being here is enough for me,' he answered. 'Now, hurry on. I want to see if you like it.'

Maria gasped as the paper finally fell away and she opened the little box within. It contained a beautiful, diamond pendant.

'Oh, Daniel! It's far, far too expensive!'

She shook her head, her dark eyes glistening with tears.

'It's really beautiful, but I can't possibly accept it. What would Rob think?'

Daniel's lips tightened, and he rose to his feet, pacing the length of the room before turning round and facing her.

'You really mean to marry him then?' he asked harshly.

'Yes, Daniel. He needs me.'

Daniel looked at her sadly, his voice little more than a whisper, so that, afterwards, Maria couldn't be quite sure whether she'd imagined his words or not.

'And what about me? Don't I need you?'

* * *

Maria tried to return Daniel's necklace to him on several occasions over the next few days, but he refused to accept it.

'Keep it, it's a gift. Don't worry, Maria, there's absolutely no strings attached whatsoever.'

And so, reluctantly, Maria had kept it. But she didn't wear it, although she took it out every night and looked at it before she went to bed.

Then the bombshell dropped.

Caroline and her husband were returning to their home on the outskirts of Chester, and Caroline had requested that her mother accompany her. She had announced to the family that she had recently discovered she was expecting her first baby, and Simon had volunteered for service overseas. He would be going out to India during the second week of January.

Rachel Pennington didn't hesitate. Of course she would go with her daughter. She considered it her duty to do so, and Maria, as her lady's maid, would naturally be expected to accompany her.

Rob was furious when Maria told him when they next met.

'I won't be gone for that long, Rob,' Maria replied, trying to soothe him.

'Now that Colonel Freestone knows about the baby, he's going to try to cut short his time in India. Mrs Pennington wouldn't be able to stay with Miss Caroline for months on end. Mr Pennington would never stand for it. I should think that it'll only be for about two months, three at the most.'

'And don't you think that's rather a long time for a couple about to be married to be apart from each other?'

His face, red with temper, loomed closer to hers, and Maria shrank away involuntarily. This was a side of Rob that she hadn't yet seen, and didn't much like.

'Mrs Pennington is to pay me extra which is quite generous of her.'

Maria was quite anxious to go, as she was feeling increasingly under strain these days. In many ways, she regretted her impulsive decision to become engaged to Rob, because she now knew that the feelings she had towards him were not true love.

She had to admit she was in love

with Daniel Pennington. Seeing him, day in, day out, was a living torment. It would be good to get away to Chester, out of sight of both Rob and Daniel. It would give her space to breathe, to think . . .

'Generous of her my foot!' Rob interrupted her train of thought. 'She's just making a convenience of you, that's all.'

'Not at all, Rob. Mrs Pennington is very fond of Caroline. You can hardly expect her to just leave her daughter all alone at a time like this. Anyway, think what the extra money will mean for us. It'll mean that I can save quite a lot more. You've always said you'd like your own home, rather than moving in with your mother. Well, this money could go towards it.'

At long last, Rob began to come round.

'Well, put like that, I suppose it does have some merits. Mind you, I'm not at all happy about being away from you for so long.'

Then he seemed to make up his mind.

'All right, Maria, you can go, but for no more than three months, mind! Any longer than that, and I will come personally and fetch you away.'

7

Maria arrived back at Pennington Hall at the end of March. Although she had been away almost three months, she still hadn't come to any decision regarding her engagement to Rob.

She had seen Daniel during these months, as he had paid a two-week visit to his sister's house in February. He had told Maria how he was now helping his father with the running of the mines, although, so far, his duties had been purely managerial, which didn't satisfy him at all. He was confined to the office.

However, Maria had only been back three days when the men went on strike. Rob himself led a deputation of men to Pennington Hall to protest about the archaic working conditions at Snaefell mine.

It was a Sunday, and the mines were

closed. Mr Pennington was at home, and Maria was in Mrs Pennington's drawing-room, writing out invitations for the Easter Ball at Pennington Hall. A fracas outside drew her attention, and she jumped to her feet and rushed over to the window. It looked down over the main entrance.

The sight which met her eyes filled her with horror. Rob was standing at the head of about forty or fifty men, hammering on the Pennington's front door. Some of the men with him were shouting loudly, and one or two even brandished sticks.

Bates, the butler, opened the door, and then quickly tried to close it again, but he was too late. Rob, accompanied by a tall, burly man, were already inside. Maria could see them both motion for the other men to remain outside.

Maria was aware that Rob was becoming increasingly discontented with the working conditions in the mines, and, in particular, the one at Snaefell. It was situated on the slopes of the island's only mountain. However, he hadn't told her he was planning to lead a deputation to the Hall, and she couldn't help but feel very angry towards him.

Marcus Pennington himself had appeared, his face pale with anger. Maria couldn't help thinking that she would have warned the Penningtons had she known about this deputation. After all, what could the men possibly hope to gain from such a confrontation?

Surely it would have been more sensible to have approached Daniel, who was now taking more interest in the mines, and was known for being much more liberal in his way of thinking than his father.

'What's the meaning of this?' Marcus Pennington demanded. 'Is this your doing, Cregeen?'

'Yes, sir, it was my idea, but the men were more than ready to come along, too.'

He thrust a paper at Marcus Pennington.

'This is a signed petition, sir, asking that you improve the working conditions at Snaefell before there's an accident. A lot of the machinery is very antiquated and . . . '

He got no further, as Marcus Pennington deliberately tore in half the paper Rob had given him, and flung it away from him.

'That's what I think of your petition, Cregeen. And you needn't bother reporting for work tomorrow, neither of you, nor Kewley here, or any of the men who have taken part in this disgraceful episode. I am the master here, and I intend to remain so. Now, get out of my house before I call the police.'

Rob stared at the master of Pennington Hall in disgust, before turning on his heel. He murmured to Kewley.

'Come on, Bill, we might as well be off. We'll get no fair hearing from this one.'

Maria stood as if turned to stone, her face devoid of colour, and her dark eyes looking enormous, as the two men departed. Marcus Pennington turned and gave her a disparaging look.

'I understand that you're engaged to be married to that young man, Miss Oates. Well, all I can say is that if you value your position here as my wife's personal maid, you would do well to think twice about actually going through with a wedding.'

Then he turned away, and walked quickly up the staircase.

Daniel had been out visiting friends and so had failed to witness the deputation to Pennington Hall. When he returned, however, his father sent for him and gave him every detail. Daniel heard him out, then immediately sought out Maria, to get her version of what had happened. They went outside.

'Did you know that Rob Cregeen was going to bring the men here, Maria?' he asked, as they walked in the extensive grounds.

Maria shook her head.

'Maybe it wasn't the correct way to

go about things,' Daniel said, 'but then, what would have been? After all, I understand that there have been several complaints made to my father already about the conditions at Snaefell mine, but he hadn't bothered to do anything about it. As far as he's concerned, they're just being militant with no just cause.'

He shook his head and Maria could sense his concern over the outcome of events.

He patted Maria's shoulder.

'But don't worry, Maria. I certainly intend to get to the bottom of all this. My father has been anxious for me to take up the position of captain of the mines for some time. Now I intend to do so. And I won't be the kind of captain who whiles his time away in the offices. I intend to go down into Snaefell mine and see for myself what working conditions are really like. If I find them lacking, then I will make Father reinstate the men, and order new equipment.'

At that moment, Rachel Pennington's imperious voice could be heard calling.

'Daniel! Maria! What are you doing?'

Her eyes narrowed as they approached her and she looked at Maria quite accusingly. 'Felicity told me that you were walking together in the gardens. Why, I wonder?'

Daniel raised his eyebrows.

'Surely taking a walk together isn't a crime, Mother?'

Rachel Pennington didn't give a direct answer, instead, she said, 'It's Maria's day off. I'm sure that she doesn't want to waste it hanging around Pennington Hall when she could be seeing that young man of hers. After all, I'm sure she and young Cregeen must have quite a lot to talk about, given this morning's unpleasant, little episode!'

Maria felt colour flare in her cheeks as she defended herself.

'I didn't know Rob meant to come here this morning, Mrs Pennington, or I would have tried to dissuade him.'

Daniel gave his mother a curt nod. 'Please excuse us. As you pointed out, it's Maria's day off, and she should be enjoying it, rather than standing here listening to the occupants of Pennington Hall's outmoded opinions!'

He took hold of Maria's arm, and led her off in the opposite direction, seemingly oblivious to his mother's glowering look.

'Daniel, where are we going?' Maria murmured nervously. 'You've angered your mother.'

'Mother will have to condition herself to moving into the twentieth century,' he replied, grinning. 'As to where we're going, well, that's your choice, just as long as you'll permit me to accompany you.'

Maria found that she was smiling back at him, but then she sobered.

'Oh, do you really think that this is being very wise? After all, Rob's been laid off, and if I continue in this vein, it's very likely that I'm going to be out of a job, too.'

'I've already told you that if Rob Cregeen's claims are valid, which I suspect they are, then I'll personally see that he, and the rest of the men, are reinstated as soon as possible.'

He eyed her consideringly.

'And as for you, young lady. Well, I think I can promise you employment with Mother while you still want it.'

Maria shook her head.

'You're very sure of yourself, aren't you?'

'Not really, but I do pride myself on knowing my parents. But let's forget them for now, and concentrate on having some time to ourselves. Shall we take the carriage, or would you rather go somewhere on the tram?'

'Oh, the tram,' Maria replied, without hesitation.

'Then the tram it'll be,' Daniel answered, smiling at her as they began walking down the long driveway away from Pennington Hall.

They headed for Douglas, and took a walk along the promenade, Maria linked to Daniel. She supposed she ought to feel guilty, but there was a curious sense of unreality about the day, and, besides, she was angry with Rob for not telling her that he planned to come up to the Hall that morning.

Neither of them had had lunch, the morning having been too disturbed, but as it was getting rather late for a mid-day meal, Daniel took Maria into one of the larger hotels where they enjoyed an elaborate afternoon tea.

It was the first time that Maria had been into the Castle Mona Hotel, and she was a little over-awed.

At that moment, her thoughts were interrupted by the arrival of an immaculately-dressed young couple at the side of their table.

'Why, Daniel, you old rogue!' the man exclaimed, a handsome, blond fellow in his twenties. 'You didn't let on that you were courting, and a very attractive, young lady she is, too. Do you mind if Arabella and I join you? It's getting pretty crowded in here, and it's much nicer having company, don't you think?'

Then, seemingly oblivious to Daniel's scowl, the gentleman sat down next to Maria, his companion sitting down next to Daniel.

'If you wish to stay, then of course you're most welcome,' Daniel said, quickly, but although he smiled, Maria noticed that the smile didn't reach his eyes. 'In any event, let me introduce you to my companion.'

He turned to Maria.

'Maria, this is the Honourable James Fortescue, and his fiancée, Miss Arabella Kerruish. James, Arabella, this is Miss Maria Oates.'

James Fortescue's brow wrinkled.

'Miss Maria Oates, eh? Strange, but I don't seem to have heard of you. Are you new to island society.'

Maria looked at him directly.

'I'm not part of it. I'm Mrs Pennington's lady's maid.'

'Oh, now I understand, old man, why our presence here can hardly have been very welcome. Come on, Arabella, I think it's probably advisable for us to find another table.'

Arabella didn't need telling twice. She was on her feet faster than Maria would have thought her full, billowing skirts would have allowed her to move.

'Nice to meet you,' she murmured, before hurrying off after her fiancé.

'I'm sorry about that, Maria.' Daniel sighed. 'I suppose I should have known that we'd be likely to run into people like them here, but it's been such a chaotic morning, that I just didn't stop to think.'

'It's the old, old story, Daniel, of the social gap. They couldn't get away quickly enough when they realised that I was just a servant.'

Daniel looked angry.

'They're of no importance, don't let them upset you. Most of the people in my family's so-called social circle tend to be very shallow, I'm afraid.'

Maria didn't doubt that was true, but, nevertheless, the arrival of James

Fortescue and Arabella had somehow managed to put a damper on the afternoon. She was quite glad when Daniel paid the bill, and they left the hotel.

'Are you coming back to the Hall, or are you going to see your mother?' he asked as they boarded the tram.

'I'd better go and see Mother. I try to call in most days I'm off, otherwise she worries that something's happened to me.' Maria smiled. 'I suppose it's silly, really, but she's always been very protective of me.'

'I don't think it's at all silly, in fact, I think it's very nice, and I can well understand why she feels like that. You tend to bring out the protective instinct in people, Maria Oates. It's part of your charm.'

'You shouldn't be saying things like that to me. After all, you're my employer's son, and I'm engaged to Rob.'

'Engagements can be broken, and social barriers can be pulled down,' he replied. 'Anyway, I rather think that Mother will have some idea of how the land lies after this morning.'

'Well, she didn't approve of me walking in the grounds with you, so I can't imagine what she'll think of you taking me out for the afternoon.'

'Don't worry, Maria, I can handle Mother. Father's a different kettle of fish, but we'll worry about him when the time comes. Anyway, as you're going to see your mother, perhaps you might allow me to accompany you. I've never had the pleasure of meeting Mrs Oates, but I'd dearly like to.'

Maria was startled.

'You want to meet my mother? Well, of course, I don't see any problem. I'm sure that she'd be delighted, in fact!'

And that Maria didn't doubt was true, as she visualised Jessie weighing up Daniel Pennington, and considering him a much more suitable partner for her daughter than Rob Cregeen!

Oh, if only it could be! But then she shook her head ruefully.

8

If Jessie was surprised when her daughter arrived with Daniel Pennington, she was astute enough not to show it. She immediately took control, which was probably just as well, as Isobel, totally overawed, was fluttering round like a nervous mother hen.

It was Jessie who showed Daniel into the parlour, a room which was normally only used at Christmas, or when guests visited the farmhouse, which wasn't very often, given Will's taciturn, and generally unpleasant, personality.

'Do sit down, Mr Pennington. Can we offer you some refreshment? Some tea and cakes, perhaps?'

'Do call me Daniel, Mrs Oates, and Maria and I have already taken afternoon tea at the Castle Mona hotel, but I'd welcome a cup of tea, if that's no trouble.'

'No, no trouble at all,' Isobel stammered from the doorway. 'I'll see to it rightaway.'

Daniel smiled warmly at Isobel.

'Thank you, Mrs Croft, that's very kind of you, but don't rush. I don't want to put you to any bother. I really only came so that I could meet Maria's mother.'

He gazed at Maria fondly.

'She often talks about you, Mrs Oates, so I thought that it would be nice to meet you. It's so much easier when one can put a face to a name.'

'And it's very nice for me to be able to meet one of the family for whom my daughter works. She's doing favourably at the Hall, I trust?'

Daniel smiled.

'Oh yes, Mrs Oates, she's doing very well indeed. In fact, I don't think that mother has ever had a lady's maid with whom she's been so satisfied. Usually she's accusing them of being inept and clumsy, but no-one could accuse Maria of such things.'

Jessie beamed.

'That's very kind of you, Mr Pen . . . er, Daniel. And what about you? Maria has been telling me that you may take over from your father at the mines.'

Colour flared into Maria's cheeks. That had been told to her mother in confidence! What on earth would Daniel think of her tittle-tattling? But he didn't seem annoyed. In fact, he looked pleased.

'I'm glad to hear that Maria's mentioned me to you, Mrs Oates,' he said. 'At least it shows she thinks about me a little.'

Oh, if only he knew just how often I do think about him, Maria thought to herself sadly.

'I must confess,' Daniel went on, 'that after I left university, I couldn't make my mind up about what I wanted to do. I thought about emigrating, in fact. I still do, but not yet.'

He looked at Maria meaningfully,

a look that was lost on her, but correctly interpreted by her mother. Jessie couldn't help but feel a surge of pride that this handsome, young gentleman was most definitely interested in her daughter.

'Maria's probably told you that I've been doing managerial work at the mines, but since the incident this morning, I've been thinking that I should be taking a much more active rôle.'

He passed a hand through his hair.

'But I'm forgetting, you won't have heard of what took place up at the Hall this morning, will you?'

Jessie shook her head, and Daniel began the account of the events at the Hall. He was still explaining to her, when Isobel came in with the tea. Jessie threw a horrified look in Maria's direction.

'Rob actually led this deputation? Oh, Maria! How could you allow him to do such a thing?'

'I didn't know anything about it until

they arrived at the Hall. He didn't tell me.'

'It's not Maria's fault,' Daniel interrupted, quickly. 'In fact, I don't blame anyone. I feel sure the men will have just cause. Perhaps what they did wasn't the wisest way of going about things, but then, my father is a very stubborn man. I suppose they felt that they had to put on a strong front to try and get him to listen.'

'And did he?' Jessie asked doubtfully.

'No, in fact they've been laid off work indefinitely.'

'That's going to cause real hardship for a lot of them, Rob's family included,' Jessie said worriedly.

'Yes, I know. I did wonder if he might get his job with the Steam Packet back.'

'I shouldn't think so,' Daniel said and his voice was dismissive. 'But don't worry. I think you'll find that they won't be out for too long. I intend to tell Father that I'll take up the position of captain of the mines, and then decisions will be up to me. I think they'll find me a much more enlightened employer than my father.'

'I'm sure they will.' Jessie smiled. 'You're a very fine man, Daniel. It's a pity there's not more like you. And now, Maria, are you staying here tonight?'

Maria hesitated, and looked at Daniel. She was wondering just how welcome she'd be at the Hall.

'Yes, I think you should stay, Maria. That way you're getting more out of your day off, and it'll also give me an opportunity to speak to Mother. Be back about nine-thirty tomorrow. That'll be early enough, seeing as Mother rarely rises before ten anyway.'

He finished his tea, and stood up.

'Well, I suppose I should be getting back.'

He extended a hand to Jessie.

'It's been very nice meeting you, Mrs Oates. I hope I may come again.'

* * *

Maria was nervous when the bell summoning her to attend Mrs Pennington sounded in her room at Pennington Hall the following day, shortly after she had returned from the farm.

Rachel Pennington was fully dressed, and sitting by her dressing-table. As Maria entered, she turned round, and smiled. But it was a very perfunctory smile, and certainly didn't reach her eyes.

'Ah, there you are, Maria. I want you to dress my hair for me. I've been invited to take lunch with Major and Mrs Downward.'

'Certainly, Mrs Pennington.'

'Tell me, Maria, have you seen that young man of yours since yesterday morning's incident?'

Maria kept her eyes downcast as she replied.

'No, ma'am.'

'Well, I'm sure you must want to

speak to him, so as I don't expect to be returning back here until around four o'clock, and won't need you with me, you can have the time off to visit the Cregeens. No doubt Robert will be at home seeing as he has been laid off.'

'Thank you, ma'am,' Maria replied, although, in truth, she wasn't at all sure that she did want to see Rob, and she wondered why Rachel Pennington was anxious for her to do so.

'Do you perhaps have something which you wish me to say to him?' she asked, tentatively.

'You could tell him that it would be in both your interests for him not to incite the men further. My husband is extremely angry about the whole affair, and I really cannot say how it will all end. But he should listen to you. After all, you are engaged to him.'

'Yes, I'll try, ma'am, although I don't really know that he'll take much notice of what I have to say in a matter like this.'

'Well, if he wants to marry you, he

should listen. Make that clear to him. He can hardly support you if all he has to live on are strike handouts. You've been engaged for around three and a half months now, haven't you?'

Maria nodded, wondering what was coming next.

'When exactly had you planned on marrying? A summer wedding would be very nice, wouldn't it? How about June? That's a traditional month for weddings.'

Maria began to understand. Mrs Pennington was frightened of Daniel's attentions towards her, and was trying to get her safely married to Rob as soon as possible.

'We haven't actually discussed a date,' she began, warily.

Mrs Pennington's dark eyes flashed with temper.

'Then I think it's about time you did, don't you, Maria?' she asked, making herself clearly understood.

However, Maria didn't discuss a wedding date with Rob when they met, partly because she didn't want to, but also because the occasion didn't really arise.

When she arrived at the Cregeen's cottage, it was to find Rob sitting out in the little, back garden with young Johnnie helping the youngster to whittle a wooden model of the island's famous water wheel.

'Why, that's beautiful!' Maria exclaimed, touched by the look of pride which spread over Johnnie's features. 'Would you mind if I held it for a moment? I promise that I'll treat it very gently.'

Johnnie extended the wood carving to Maria, who took it gently.

'It's absolutely perfect,' she exclaimed. 'Is this the first one you've done?'

'Yes, but I plan to do more, and paint them in the great wheel's colours of red, white and black. Rob's going to help me seeing as he's no work, and Ma's going to sell them from the window of her little café. I reckon they should sell well in the season.'

'I'm sure they will,' Maria agreed. 'Just make sure that you don't sell them too cheaply.'

Rob, she noticed, still hadn't said a word.

'I've got a couple of hours off this afternoon,' she said, addressing Rob. 'Perhaps you'd like to come out for a walk with me, or are you too busy?' Rob looked at Johnnie.

'Do you think you can manage to finish the whittling while I'm away?'

'Of course I can,' Johnnie answered with a laugh. 'After all, I've had plenty of experience, carving Manx cats, Manx fairies, and the like!'

Rob nodded glumly.

'Yes, you're better than me, young Johnnie, aren't you? Still, you'll have to try and teach your old brother a trick or two now that he's been tossed out on to the scrap heap work wise, so to speak.'

'I can tell you, Maria, that this fellow has been like a bear with a sore head since the deputation up to the Hall went all wrong,' Johnnie said.

'I'm sure there's no need for him to be,' Maria replied, soothingly. 'After all, it's very early days yet. Just wait until Daniel takes over as captain, then there'll be some changes.'

'Oh, so it's Daniel now, is it? Well, let me tell you this! I heard from one of the boys that you were out with the Pennington's son, dining in that fancy Castle Mona yesterday afternoon. I won't stand for the likes of that from the woman I'm engaged to be married to. Do you understand?'

9

As she got ready for bed that night in her room at the Hall, Maria reflected that the afternoon had been far from the happy success she had hoped it would be.

She had won Rob round to a degree, in so much as he had apologised for his jealousy of Daniel Pennington, and admitted that the latter was a much better man than his father, Marcus Pennington. But even so, she couldn't help but feel that a rift was forming between her and Rob.

To a large extent, it was probably her own fault, her own guilt, in fact, that she realised now that she cared more for the Pennington's only son that she did her betrothed. It made her feel ashamed of herself, because she knew that Rob was a good, hard-working man, even if he did possess a quick temper, something which she hadn't seen when he had worked for the Steam Packet Company.

If she was a loyal fiancée, she would try to be more patient, try harder to understand him. And she would forget Daniel Pennington! For, despite what her mother might think, Maria knew that there could never be any future for them.

Her mind was still in a complete turmoil as Maria eventually finished plaiting her hair, and turned out the lamp. But sleep eluded her, and after an hour's tossing and turning, she gave up and put the lamp on again.

Although she had read it at least once before, Emily Bronte's 'Wuthering Heights' had always been one of her favourite novels. She took out her copy from a drawer in the cabinet by her bed, and began reading it once again. The powerful love story held her attention, and Maria had re-read much of the book when she eventually switched off the lamp after three o'clock.

She didn't immediately hear Mrs

Pennington's buzzer sounding for her the following morning as a result. When it eventually penetrated her state of half-wakefulness, she leaped out of bed in some alarm, glancing at the clock on the dresser.

It was almost ten o'clock, and she wasn't even dressed! At this rate, she was certainly asking to be dismissed!

What should she do, she wondered desperately — get dressed, and have the buzzer sounding again, or don her dressing-gown and hurry over to Mrs Pennington's room to apologise for her tardiness.

In the end, the buzzer's shrill sound decided for her. She would have to go to Mrs Pennington in her dressing-gown. She had only covered a yard or so when she had the misfortune to come face to face with Marcus Pennington, who stopped in his tracks, eyeing her in amazement.

'Miss Oates, what on earth are you doing wandering around my house in a state of undress?'

'I'm very sorry, sir, but you see, I overslept, and your wife has been buzzing for me.'

He looked her up and down disparagingly.

'I cannot have you wandering around the house and attending my lady wife in such a manner! Go back to your room and make yourself presentable as quickly as possible. I shall tell my wife that you overslept.'

'Thank you, sir. I'm sorry,' Maria murmured.

Marcus Pennington put a hand to his head.

'Oh, just get on your way, girl! I honestly don't know why Mrs Pennington insists on keeping you. Personally, I would have you dismissed like that disreputable fellow whom my fool of a son is currently endeavouring to get reinstated at the mine! Now, get out of my sight!'

Maria didn't need telling twice. Without another word, she hurried back to the sanctuary of her room, and hurriedly changed into her gown, quickly fastening her hair in a bun. Rachel Pennington actually looked quite amused when Maria arrived in her room several minutes later.

'Well, you've managed to upset my husband, Maria. What have you got to say about that, eh?'

'I'm very sorry, ma'am. I certainly didn't mean to offend him, and I'm very sorry for my lateness this morning. I just couldn't get off to sleep last night, and I'm afraid that I ended up reading a good part of the night.'

Rachel Pennington motioned for Maria to sit down.

'Really, it must have been a most interesting book. Do tell me, Maria, what it was that you were reading.'

' 'Wuthering Heights', ma'am. It's a very powerful story.'

'Indeed, yes, of hopeless love, if I recall rightly.' Rachel Pennington's eyes narrowed. 'Do you perhaps hanker after a hopeless love, Maria?'

'I don't know what you mean, Mrs

Pennington,' Maria replied, her voice scarcely more than a whisper, as she knew very well to what her employer referred.

'Oh, don't play the innocent with me, Maria Oates. I know very well that my errant son is infatuated with you. What I want to know is if you share his feelings.'

'I realise that Mr Daniel comes from a different social standing, and I will always respect that. Anyway, aren't you forgetting the fact that I'm engaged to be married to Robert Cregeen?'

Maria was surprised at how calm her voice sounded, for she was trembling inside.

'I don't forget it,' Rachel Pennington replied. 'I just hope that you will continue to remember it!'

During the next few weeks, Daniel won his way, and the men were reinstated in the mines a fortnight after Easter.

He had gone down into both the Laxey and Snaefell mines, but whilst he had found the conditions in Laxey mines acceptable, if not ideal, he had declared that Snaefell mines were an absolute disgrace.

Needless to say, Marcus Pennington had been appalled by his son's findings, and had demanded that an independent body should look into the conditions in the Snaefell mines before he would give his permission for new equipment to be ordered. Daniel had been only too happy to agree.

One evening, soon after, Maria was surprised to receive a visit from Daniel, in her own room.

She opened the door to his knock and looked at him in surprise.

'What on earth are you doing here?' she demanded. 'If anyone should see you there'll be terrible trouble.'

'Then we'll just have to make sure that they don't, won't we?' he said, grinning.

He pushed past her into the room, and sat down, uninvited, on her bedside chair.

'Actually, I only came to tell you that Father had some people look at the equipment in Snaefell mine today, and they thought, like me, that it was hopelessly out of date. He's had no option but to agree to my ordering some new stuff.'

Maria clapped her hands.

'Oh, that is good news. I'm really glad. Mind you, I'd love to have seen the expression on your father's face when they told him.'

'I can assure you, it was a study,' Daniel told her, laughing. Then he became serious. 'The only problem is that it takes quite a while to get things shipped over to the island. I shouldn't think that we'll have the new things until June at the very earliest.'

'Oh, well, at least they'll be coming, and it's not that long until June now, just over a month.'

'Yes, that's true, and at least they'll be here for the coming winter. That's usually the hardest time for the mine workers.'

He stood up.

'Oh, well, much as I don't want to, I suppose I'd better go. After all, even I am at a loss to know how I'd explain my presence in your room to Papa!'

10

For Maria, Monday, May the tenth, started the same as any other. She had been summoned to Rachel Pennington's room, and had duly dressed her employer's hair in readiness for a shopping expedition into Douglas.

But they never reached the town. Shortly after half past ten, there was a sharp knock at Rachel Pennington's door. Before she had a chance to give the call to enter, the door burst open, and a white-faced Marcus Pennington burst into the room.

'Marcus! What on earth is the meaning of this?' his wife had demanded. 'Surely you should still be at work. You're not ill, are you? You're very pale.'

Marcus Pennington sank into the nearest chair as if his legs would no longer hold him up.

'There's been an accident,' he said eventually. 'A very bad one, very bad indeed, at the Snaefell mine.'

Maria's hand flew to her mouth, and she stifled a cry. Marcus Pennington lifted dull eyes to her.

'There's a number of fatalities, I'm afraid. We don't know exactly who as yet, but only ten miners managed to make their way back up.'

'Was . . . was Rob among them?' Maria asked, her voice sounding as if it came from a long way away, as a picture of Mrs Wheeler's prophecy came into her mind.

Marcus Pennington shook his head. 'No,' he whispered. 'He wasn't.'

Then he turned anguished eyes to his wife.

'And Daniel, impetuous, young fool that he is, has gone down there, into that fume-filled pit to look for survivors.'

But Maria was no longer listening. The room was starting to disintegrate around her, and she felt herself starting to fall, and then, nothing, but blessed oblivion.

The next few days held a quality of unreality for Maria. She couldn't bring herself to come to terms with the fact that Rob had perished in the mine. Even when Daniel sought her out later that awful day and told her, as kindly as possible, that Rob and the other men hadn't suffered, Maria still reacted as though all that was happening around her was a bad dream.

'I'm so very, very sorry, Maria,' Daniel said, taking in her white face, and dark, sad eyes. 'It should never have happened, and the only consolation I can give you is to tell you that Rob would have known very little about it.'

Maria looked up at him angrily.

'How can you possibly imagine how he must have felt down there, when he knew that he was trapped, left to rot so that landowners like you can continue with your idle, selfish lives!'

'I wouldn't have had it happen for

anything,' Daniel replied, his face pale. 'I had fought to improve conditions at the mine. I never thought that . . . '

'Landowners never do think, that's the trouble!'

Maria left him standing there, ignoring his hoarse cry of, 'Maria, wait, please!'

But she hadn't been able to talk to him. He was alive, and Rob Cregeen, her fiancé, was dead. The fact that she knew that she hadn't cared for Rob as much as a fiancée should, didn't help, and it soon became clear to Maria that she couldn't go on working at Pennington Hall, serving the family who had brought about Rob's death.

On the third day following the accident, Maria left Pennington Hall before the family was about. She had packed her small suitcase the previous evening, having made her mind up about what she must do. She would go back to Croft farm, and offer to help out there until she could find alternative employment.

It was only as the tram was winding

it's way through the countryside that she allowed herself to face the very real possibility that Will Croft wouldn't give his permission for her to stay. After all, there was no love lost between her and her brother. But what alternative did she have?

She'd saved a little money, and could pay for lodgings for a short time, but only a short time, and, besides, she felt that she needed Jessie's comforting presence at a time when her whole world had been turned upside down.

Her mother had visited her on the day of the disaster, but at that time, Maria had still been in a state of shock, and unresponsive. Jessie had returned to the farm, telling her daughter that she would look forward to seeing her on her next day off.

Perhaps that would be the best thing to say at first, at least to Will — that the Penningtons had decided to give her a few days off to get over the shock. He would believe that, and, heartless as he undoubtedly was, would be very unlikely to turn her away if he thought her stay was temporary.

Maria was quite winded as she entered the farmyard, and, unfortunately for her, ran into her brother just coming out of the farmhouse to start his day's work.

'What the devil are you doing here? And with that case in your hand, too!' Will's eyes narrowed.

'The Penningtons have given me several days off to get over my bereavement,' Maria replied coldly.

Will moved away from the door.

'That was mighty charitable of them, seeing as how they didn't even know that you had anywhere to go. Well, I suppose you'd better come in. But mind you don't stay too long. I'm not a charitable organisation.'

Will was already walking away, his mind on the farm work, as Maria turned towards the door. She received a much warmer welcome from her mother, Isobel and the children.

'Come along now, children, let me get you ready for school,' Isobel said, ushering the young Crofts out of the room, pausing in the doorway.

'I'm really sorry about Rob, Maria, and you're welcome to stay just as long as you want to, no matter what Will says.'

Maria smiled her thanks, before embracing her mother. To her dismay, tears began to course freely down her cheeks. Jessie patted her head.

'There, let it out, Maria. Don't try to bottle it all up. That only makes things worse.'

'Oh, Mother, I feel so guilty,' Maria moaned. 'I didn't really want to marry Rob, but I certainly didn't want him dead.'

'There, there. I know you didn't, love. But time's a great healer. Just you wait and see!'

Jessie told Will that evening that Maria would in fact be staying at the farm until she found another job.

'What? You expect me to keep that

great lump of a girl! Well, I swear I . . .'

'Oh, stop blustering, Will. She's my daughter, and she's staying here!'

Will opened and shut his mouth. He wasn't used to anyone talking back to him.

'Well, if she's to stay here, she'll have to earn her keep,' he blurted out.

'I'll be only too happy to do so,' Maria replied.

In the next few days, Maria found that she was so tired when she actually got to bed that she managed to fall asleep immediately. However, she was suffering from nightmares, where she felt herself choking on acrid black smoke, and then she would see Rob's face, and his arms reaching out to her, but she was always too far away from him. Then it all faded away, and she would wake up, trembling.

When she told her mother, Jessie insisted that she see Dr Rogers, who prescribed a mild sedative for her to take before going to bed. Maria was reluctant to take it at first, but Jessie managed to persuade her to try it, and she found that it did help to keep the distressing dreams at bay.

Daniel called on Maria's second day at the farm, but she refused to see him. After all, what good could possibly come out of it? It would only reawaken old memories, and make her feel even worse. There couldn't possibly be any future for them together, now.

But Maria reckoned without Daniel's persistence, and, one sunny morning when she was out in the fields transplanting some young cabbages, she heard his voice behind her. Straightening up, she turned round and glared at him.

'How did you know I was working out here?' she demanded, brusquely.

'Isobel told me.'

'Trust Isobel! She's always trying to be helpful. Well, what do you want?'

Daniel looked at her pointedly, before speaking.

'You, Maria. I want you,' he said gently.

'Me? What do you mean?'

'I love you, Maria. I think I always have, from the first moment I set eyes on you.

'After the Snaefell mining disaster, I no longer feel that I wish to stay here on the island. I think I mentioned before that I've contemplated emigrating. Well, this has made up my mind.'

He took a deep breath.

'Maria, will you do me the honour of becoming my wife and emigrating to South Africa with me?'

Maria stared at him in bewilderment.

'You really mean it, don't you?' she murmured eventually.

'Yes,' he replied.

She shook her head.

'I won't pretend that I'm not tempted, but it's far too soon, and we haven't really spent that much time together. If we're going to think about spending the rest of our lives with one another, then I think that we should take some time to get to know each other better.'

He smiled ruefully.

'Well, it's better than a downright refusal, I suppose! All right, Maria Oates, if that's what you want, then I'll begin to court you.'

It soon became known in the small island community that Maria and Daniel were courting. They were absolutely furious, and Maria received one threatening letter from Marcus Pennington, followed by a conciliatory one from his wife, which attempted to buy her off.

'Mother, it's intolerable!' she cried, after that particular incident. 'What on earth can I do? I'm starting to feel like a social outcast.'

'This island is not the place for you and Daniel. It won't let you forget the past, or the fact that you're from different backgrounds. No, much as it breaks my heart to say it, I think, if you love him, which I'm sure you do, then you should agree to marry him and go out to South Africa. Make new lives for yourselves.'

Maria hesitated.

'But what about you, Mother?'

Jessie smiled.

'Don't worry about me. I've had the best part of my life, whereas yours is still in front of you. Besides, I've grown very fond of Isobel and the children. And I do believe I've learned to handle Will as well. No, Maria, I'll be all right. You go and grasp happiness when it's offered to you.'

That night, Daniel and Maria took the tram into Ramsey and had dinner in a cosy, little restaurant overlooking the harbour.

'Daniel, I've got something to tell you,' Maria said.

'You have? Good, I hope? After all, we seem to have had more than our fair share of problems recently.'

Maria bit her lip.

'Yes, that's true, which is one reason why I've reached my decision. Daniel, I want to go to South Africa with you if you feel you love me enough to oppose your parents' disapproval.'

'You know I do,' he replied. 'But tell me, what other reasons were instrumental in making you decide?'

'I'm finding it increasingly difficult to live without you,' she murmured, in a voice so low that Daniel wasn't sure whether he'd imagined her words or not.

'I really think we should leave as soon as possible, my dearest,' he said, reaching across the table and taking her hand in his. 'After all, things have hardly been easy for you these past weeks.'

'They haven't been easy for you, either,' Maria replied, 'I shouldn't have blamed you for the mining disaster. You did all you could, and I've always known that.'

She smiled sadly.

'Actually, I don't think I was blaming you at all. I think I was really blaming myself because after I'd met you, I realised that I wasn't in love with poor Rob. I just didn't know what to do about it, particularly after his father died and he was so upset.'

'Which was why you got engaged to him,' Daniel interrupted.

Maria nodded.

'Yes, but it was rather foolish of me really, wasn't it?'

'It showed that you have a very kind nature, which is one of the reasons why I love you,' he replied, smiling at her tenderly. 'But it's no good dwelling on the past,' Daniel continued. 'That's why I feel we should leave here just as soon as we can, and make a new start.'

He looked slightly embarrassed as he reached into his jacket pocket and took out two steam packet tickets for Liverpool.

'I purchased these some days ago in the hope that you'd agree with my plans. They're open tickets, so we can go just as soon as you're ready.'

'I understand that there's a boat

going every day,' Maria answered with a loving smile.

'Yes,' he replied, signalling for the waiter to bring the bill. 'How much time will you need?'

'Very little,' Maria replied. 'In fact, after I made my decision, I packed my case.'

Daniel was smiling as he paid the bill.

'Then tomorrow's sailing's not too soon?' he asked, as they stood up to leave.

'No,' Maria said, softly. 'After all, we've wasted enough time already.

THE END

Other titles in the Linford Romance Library

SAVAGE PARADISE
Sheila Belshaw

For four years, Diana Hamilton had dreamed of returning to Luangwa Valley in Zambia. Now she was back — and, after a close encounter with a rhino — was receiving a lecture from a tall, khaki-clad man on the dangers of going into the bush alone!

PAST BETRAYALS
Giulia Gray

As soon as Jon realized that Julia had fallen in love with him, he broke off their relationship and returned to work in the Middle East. When Jon's best friend, Danny, proposed a marriage of friendship, Julia accepted. Then Jon returned and Julia discovered her love for him remained unchanged.

PRETTY MAIDS ALL IN A ROW

Rose Meadows

The six beautiful daughters of George III of England dreamt of handsome princes coming to claim them, but the King always found some excuse to reject proposals of marriage. This is the story of what befell the Princesses as they began to seek lovers at their father's court, leaving behind rumours of secret marriages and illegitimate children.

THE GOLDEN GIRL

Paula Lindsay

Sarah had everything — wealth, social background, great beauty and magnetic charm. Her heart was ruled by love and compassion for the less fortunate in life. Yet, when one man's happiness was at stake, she failed him — and herself.